ENTERPRISING WOMEN

ENTERPRISING
WOMEN

An Entertainment

JOHN FRASER

AESOP Modern Fiction
Oxford

AESOP Modern Fiction
An imprint of AESOP Publications
Martin Noble Editorial / AESOP
28 Abberbury Road, Oxford OX4 4ES, UK
www.aesopbooks.com

www.johnfraser.info

A catalogue record of this book is
available from the British Library.

ISBN: 978-0-9927588-7-5

Contents

1 The Flies

Sophie & Stella

It's like long ago – little crowds harangued by orators.

'Blood. The imperative of revolutionary violence.' The guy's determined. Could be from Québec. The French, revolutionaries, still in America? We listen impassively.

'You don't agree?' he shouts at me, in a come-on way. Why am I here, wandering round the city? – cities are like this, always a bunch of guys, impassioned, shaking you from your drift.

'It's true,' I say. 'That's what occurs. Blood – and sometimes revolution.'

'No, no, my friend,' he says, and knows he's won. 'Permanent. Per-man-ent. Revolution! It's not a room that you unlock, and there, it's full of roasted peahens, hot and waiting for you. Chairs as well. Create, cast down! Overthrow – then overthrow again.'

I say again, sidling away, 'It's true. It's just I don't want down that road.'

'It's true,' he mocks expansively. 'And yet this guy, he'd rather go another way. What's truth, then?'

*

'Here's novelty! I've found a little cycle that fruits cash. Economics! You gotta pedal! I'm doing rather well' – my old friend Pedro. Sitting back.

I'm not doing well. I say, 'The girl I'm with, she brings the food.'

Pedro laughs, 'I bet she squawks, when she must sub you! You straight guys, and your sex!'

He used to box, now he's slumped and rubbery, slippery like a Turkish wrestler all oiled up.

'I call it the anarchy of commodities,' he says. 'You'll have seen the logic of the Strip. Architects and planners – they love the Strip, it justifies their chaos. Banal boxes, shacks, kids selling air at intersections; mules and Mercurys. But it functions. Not liberal, not progressive. No hope, no plan – just turnover. No charity. Selling what I'm asked. As long as they ask me. Washing iguanas, organising heists, spying on lovers. It all comes in, people all desperate – a buzz, a rush.'

I say, 'So it's not economics. It's chance. As long as they ask.'

'Always, that's how it is,' he says. 'If they ask – is the key. To most everything.'

I tell Pedro about my brush with truth, the militant guy. 'Yes, yes,' he says, 'of course it's true. Not that you need to bother with it. It's like I say – the women feed the warriors. You're just a parasite – they feed you just the same.' He laughs.

'The blood,' I say. 'Where it falls, what happens then? What springs up? Flowers? Nothing? Warriors?'

'These people,' Pedro says. 'Trots. They're like my friends – they went to law school, then got jobs with unions. First, the union fought for justice: then my lawyer friends discovered – they must defend the union against its members. Grievances, the guys complain – "you go so slow", "you're office bums" – you know. Chaos. Then some guy discovers some kind of pattern in it all. But still it's chaos.' He gets up, lets a fly out of the room. There's still more left.

'You see,' he says. 'Your trouble is, for you, it's all first person. You think it's all for you. But chaos comes first. And last. It doesn't care about you, your eyes, your vision, or your making sense. There's logic in it all, for sure, like – the women bring the food to feed the warriors. I'm not misogynist. Whoever brings the food is women; who gets fed – is warrior. Me – I don't go down that road.'

That's why we're friends, I guess, not going down the roads.

'Here's Adnan,' says Pedro. 'He lives here. He's a refugee. So, he does the risky stuff that might involve running. Tell my friend what you are,' he says to Adnan, 'why they're after you.'

'Which lot?' asks Adnan, anxious to please. 'Some guys love to fry their brothers, others to spy at them in cells. I can't explain. It's odd.'

'Indeed it is,' says Pedro expanding, 'but at the same time, it's not, so we don't waste time over it.'

'Purity is what you need,' says Adnan, 'the core, the diamond, the pressure. You might say there's a void, but you have to grasp – the space. Nothing in the universe is empty – between great clods of matter, distance, energies, there's what is left, what it's all about. A space, the still place where everything has ended and begun ... Space infinitely small or vast – it's both, it's all the same.'

He doesn't say it's God, the start and end, the nothing giving birth and burying. Maybe that's not what he means.

Pedro's impatient, and he says, 'Yes, yes. But people don't believe in that! They want the flying donkeys, miraculous dinners, throwing the stones, raising the dead. Now, that is something! That, I warm to – so does everybody else. Who'd love a diamond you can't see? All the things you'd hope are round the corner ... well, they are: over and over ... Someone tells about them, tall stories, till you hear, up there, the wings and hooves.'

'These flies ...' I say.

'Of course,' says Pedro, indifferent. 'We don't want cash. We want indebtedness. Eggs for life. Onions for ever. Kind! People pay cash they can't afford, and pass along. What use is that?'

'That's how we lived,' says Adnan, 'payment in kind. It's called a family. Avoid it. They send you out to fight.'

'Not me,' and Pedro laughs. 'Haven't you seen the horns and tail? The flies? I'm quite unfit for service.'

'It's that stuff,' says Adnan. 'The rutabagas – they attract.' There's a pile of white and green and yellow, more knobbly vegetables than you would want to eat.

Pedro goes into another room, there's parleying, some woman just come in. And clucking. He says, 'No, I don't want them live. Nor dead – just don't you dare. Life! Surely you can leave me some of that? Or coca leaves. There's lots that like to chew. I don't. They're for the mountains. We're not high up here, but it will come.'

Adnan says to me, 'You know – he drove around my country. I'm not a proper refugee. He picked me up, and brought me here. He studies me.'

10

I say, 'He doesn't seem the type.'

'It's all about the project – talking about himself. No constituted authorities, just doing things that's singular. And so, you reach the universal.'

'It sounds magnificent,' I say, not much convinced.

'Well, that's the project,' Adnan says. 'What is the human being? Probably not magnificent. He says "What we love today, tomorrow we may not love at all. That's the paradox – it proves my other case – that everything's dispersed, disordered. Repressed, coerced." That's what he saved me from – the power of others. That makes me a refugee. It makes us all.'

'He does all this by talking, talking about himself?' I ask.

'Leave nothing out, and always tell the truth. People will think it's lies, and you – a poor fool. Trudging to a natural death, alone, alone, still talking.'

'Is that all?' I ask. 'The rescue?'

'You mean sex? I don't imagine so. No one travels for that now.'

'You guys,' I say. 'Back there. You might have had democracy – just wait and suffer, there it comes.'

'No, no,' says Adnan. 'What comes after that. Not democracy. What Pedro says is freedom.'

'To me, it just seems capitalism,' I say.

'To you, maybe,' says Adnan, put out, 'You have to follow arguments, not cut them short. With spite.'

Pedro comes back. 'Goddam fowl,' he says. 'Can't keep them here, alive or dead. And that's a flaw. Live things – my system starts to smell of rot. Poor beasts. A nuisance to us all.'

It seems we are a fruiterers. Pedro's uneasy, says, 'Of course, I had a group, when we all had one. Those record covers!

11

Much better than the sounds, and now – that's gone. Of course, I couldn't play – but I could shake.'

We contemplate, and then he says, 'Crowds and power. All that. And then – forced to be free. I saw him, Adnan, sitting on a rock. Seated calm and contemplating – I drove my Lotus up, and thought, "What a coincidence. I'll save one guy from being swept up, lost like a bubble in champagne, forfeiting for ever, something irrevocable…"'

We look at him, expecting that he'll tell us what that lost thing is, but no, of course, that is the point – you put a name on it when it's forever lost and gone. If you had it to hand – it would just be you.

Adnan says, 'Lotus is good – but it wasn't, and not a rock.'

Something's tattooed on the inside of Pedro's wrist: 'poker'? 'popeye'? He could have been a star, a very great one. But he loves himself, just as he is, and didn't want to be bizarre, I guess. He puts his hand on Adnan's shoulder, showing him off: 'My brother, my comrade,' he says, and Adnan says, like a chorus, 'My brother, my comrade. No tie, no project. My brother…'

I go back to Sophie's place: she says, 'Off at your hen party again?'

'No,' I say. 'Whenever I leave this place, I go looking for a job.' I open a window, shout 'Kitty, kitty!' 'You see, when I'm here, I guard the property.' We have no cat.

'Don't let those fucking flies in,' Sophie shouts. 'The window!'

I say, 'I auditioned today as a salamander. Opera House. The costume was too hot.'

She's not listening. She shouts, 'Get your papers! Then a job. There's scaffolders – those high buildings. A hard hat might suit.'

'Not high,' I say. 'There's the impulse to cast down.'

'Maybe it's destiny,' she says. 'Up high, they chew those coca leaves. And, until you get your papers, no more sex.'

No price at all.

'I don't know where they'd send me back to,' I say: 'Besides, that's about guys they don't want, not countries that'll have them. Us refugees.'

'You provoked them, someone,' she says. 'Or maybe it's all lies. Paranoia.'

'Maybe,' I say.

I think, *I fell off the mad donkey: tired of obeying, going where it told me. There I was, back there in the dragon's cave. The dragon says it's a good place, homely: 'Look at all the virgins, lining up outside,' he says. 'You're the proof I'm good. I won't eat you. You're too stringy.' You start thinking how to save yourself.*

I tell Sophie, 'The police picked me out.'

'Nonsense,' she says. 'No one cares about guys like you. The dragon's dead, where you came from. The line of virgins – that still waits. There's lots of combat going on, of course.'

'I told them I'd no record,' I go on. 'They said that everyone has one. "We know all about you," this guy said. He told me, "Call me Toopip. Lieutenant. You're the presence of an absence, a space, and under pressure. A gap. You stand out. Of course, you have a record: you're unknown. Even playing noisy music, you've not been reported ... You're not natural."

'"No," I said. "I can't stand music. I prefer my own, my silent thoughts." Then they enrolled me, Sophie. I work for them, and they ignore me – it's a deal. They said, "Aren't you curious about your friends, Pedro, Adnan? Their activity?"'

"'No, not at all,' I said. 'Toopip said to travel, go to their homes, where they came from: enquire and quiz.'

'It's quite unsafe,' says Sophie. 'And the language?'

'I didn't think about the language. And it's safe. I'd be in the police.'

I tell Pedro, 'I've a task – to investigate your origins.'

'This Toopip,' he asks, 'what's he? A Thai? A Turk? The thing is this – food and water. You need those. We eat the swedes. The rest just lies, stagnates. Maybe use it as a fuel ... Those Chinese guys – the Great Helmsmen – they all had plots. Up at dawn from lonely beds to care for lettuces, cucumbers too. There is an end to that as well. Then you go, you plough up Africa, water from the poles. You bend the future, but ... And you,' he waves a hand at me, 'you're to go to where we came from, Adnan and me. Those places are quite hard, you know. A guy could lose his breath.'

'For my purposes,' I say, drawing up some height, 'the boundaries must shift. Strife, armed and not – that cannot interpose. If I must, I'll empty countries, elasticise the frontiers, twist the laws. Decontextualise, that's the word. I'll do my work, whatever costs arise.'

'Hmmm,' says Pedro. 'That Sophie. A good person – all she touches turns to grit. Not diamond dust, between you two – it's ground-up rock. You want to live – she wants to give you tasks and reasons.'

'You don't know her,' I say.

'I don't need to, if I'm right,' he says. 'Grit. It's not intuition, this gift I have. When you master something down and down, you empty it. Whether it's Zen or Nietzsche – or you and

Sophie – my certain knowing leads to the disaster. In the end, all that's outside and strange, it goes inside, subjectified. No more the world, about itself – it's just become my knowledge, personal – I've sucked them in, the masters and the trivial – I've emptied them. They're shells of dragonflies ...'

'Yes, yes,' I interrupt. 'But if you tell me all your sins, or what you've done – I'll spare myself a journey, please Toopip as well. And what a favour I have done for you, and Adnan too – to say you're being spied on and suspected ...'

He's not pleased. Indeed, he's angry. He says, 'I'm sure I've seen the title – maybe by Euripides or such – *The Flies*. The name is good. People get tired of living always in the shadow of the dark bird – wings, always wings, they make the breeze unceasing, wheesh of air on feather – "Away, the shadow! Show us the whole damn bird," they cry. You see, they want to see their sins – but sins are not the eagle, they're the flies. They multiply, they cast no shadow. In and out the house, the hut, the palace – always round, some circling, others crapping in your food ... Were I a Frenchman living in America – I'd call for revolution too! But revolution isn't half of it – however difficult it seems, that is the easy road. From darkness into light. But there's no light. There's flies,' and he waves towards the dead and dying vegetables, stacked where guys have dumped them: 'The more they come, the more they bring the flies. The less you want to eat them.'

Where does this leave me?

I say, 'Rescuing people. That should count as a good.' I'm uncertain. Their destinies, changed utterly.

'My country,' says Pedro, 'is clay. But not the kind you make men from – it's cooked. Cooked earth. If you break it, it doesn't mend. Little ovens, full of bones. Some of them yours.'

'I think you can repair that stuff ...' I say.

'No. None of your bricolage!' he shouts. 'Broke is broke. Even the flutes is broke.'

'Here's your bag packed,' says Sophie.

'No, no,' I say. 'No need. Everyone has stuff everywhere.'

'Your passport, then?' she laughs, 'or do you have a gun, shoot your way in?'

'Pedro said he'd seen my bones – those little ovens everywhere, like tiny bomb shelters in the scrub,' I say.

'I'll miss you so,' she says. 'What luck, iguana sandwiches and mescal. Day of the dead. All that.'

I say, 'What can Pedro have done, I wonder? I'll go and get his blessing,' and I do.

'Remember those ovens,' Pedro says. 'For me, it was like this. The dust, the black trees in black woods, the leaves are spikes of salt, the snot-green lizards, terrified – the coppery huts, earth stuck in the earth. You crawl inside – imagine! the heat, bowls of brown steam. The silent people, crouched around, and to his ear, the head guy has a hollow pole that's sunk into the ground. What does he hear? – why, it's the rumbling sound the earth makes as it turns. The Galileo axle – makes the world stand, a wobbly upright. Outside, there's bands of Indians, of miners, marching up and down – and there's a city, tiny, pink and orange, a procession, great images to carry round – they make you take the weight, there's scores of bearers, uniform in brown and white, all sweat and hats of thorn, above there's some madonna, clay, of course, a shapeless creature, could be boar or badger ... And do they sacrifice us all? We're forced down by the weight, there's guys on balconies, up to the sky, all shouting, throwing flowers, and goddam music from those horns ... we cannot move. We're dying, crushed. Oh no – now there are whips ... we're done, we're finished. Next thing – guns and machetes – and I shout, "No more!"

'I had to take some guy away, to rescue one, from all this weight, this life pressed down ... where can we go? Nowhere, it seems, there is no other place. They don't want to come, they know there's nowhere I can take them, there's only my desire – it fails against inertia, their gravity – they can't arise. The only way, the only exit – well, you know, it's written by those Jesuits – they know, the people know – the only way is death ...

'So there, you understand. What can you do? You save some guy – the only way is death. You understand?'

'No,' I say, 'not really. So, you didn't rescue anyone that time?'

I wait, I go on: 'If I go there, will it be like that – those long clay listening tubes, earth grinding as it turns?'

'Ah yes,' he says, 'the Galileo axle.' He turns the television on: there's girls in twos and men in knots. A dusty, sandy town. All are on foot – but no, a cart on rubber tires, my! that's a fine horse. The screen says Diyarbakir.

'Yes!' I say. 'That is my world – donkeys, mules, and people walking up and down.'

'That isn't now,' says Pedro. 'And it isn't anything to do with Adnan. It's a moment – watching that tape, brings me peace and comradeship. Like it should have been. Before the shooting. Not my fight, of course.'

'So, if I go there, it won't be at all like that?' I ask.

'To get an answer, you must have a question,' Pedro says. 'And then that's just the start. You go to places – places aren't objective. Nor are you. It's people glimpsed, underneath the boundaries ...'

'Like all you guys, squashed under the machine, the float, madonna – the flowers, the blood,' I say, and Pedro laughs – 'Yes, the party with the dead.'

'Well,' I say, 'I'll go. It's in my contract,' and he shrugs. He says, 'Remember, I know nothing of those people. Mountain Turks, they're called. People – they want strange things. "I never wanted anything but the world," as the song says.'

'You're tough to grasp,' I say. 'Maybe Sophie, protecting me, all that, has simplified my brain.'

'Protect? From what? I don't see the armoured man in you,' says Pedro.

Adnan says, 'Wherever you go, and meet – just tell them I'm in wholesale.'

'This is Stella,' Sophie says. 'She'll give you some advice.'

I say, 'I thought I'd get a send-off – party-girls, perhaps.'

'Well,' Sophie says. 'You could get pissed – but that won't help your cause.'

Stella looks like she could be employed in something – no slogans on her shirt, and in her mouth, no gum, there's just her tongue: she says,

'Your mission – finding out what's been done wrong. You know, the wrong implies there is a right ...'

I interrupt, 'It's not like that at all,' I say, and she insists, 'Of course it is – unless you're using language in a different way.'

18

'I know what's right,' I say. 'Until it all gets complicated. Then, I'm like the rest.'

Stella's impatient, and she says, 'You can't go travelling to find what you already know. The point is this – to find what you can escape from, and what you must carry on your back until you drop. There's what you escape from, and – oh no! you find that thing has popped up once again, circling round, and bars your path. Where is this garden, full of loosestrife, cratered, padlocked – where is this refuge that you've sought? Who do you rescue, when do you rescue them? – when they embark upon their cruise, or when the sharks are round? See – before you go, you have to sort it out. And maybe think it's best to stay at home.'

I'm most impressed. I say, 'Stella, my dear – it isn't party time, and I've not drunk – but come with me, we'll trip together, you can set my thinking straight ...'

'No, no,' she says, as lovely people do, 'I wouldn't think of it. I don't go with boys like you. To say your level's elementary insults the other levels reaching up and up, into invisibility,' and so she lets me know that she's up there, invisible. She stares at me as though she's stuffed.

'Well,' says Sophie, 'I knew you'd like her. Her body, at least. And that's a lot of what's going.' Sophie gives me a present – it's a tin globe of the world.

'How'd I carry this?' I ask.

'It's not for carrying, it's for consulting,' she says. 'When you know where you are, you can see in reference to wherever else.'

'I wanna be your bubble-gum bitch,' the radio's singing. Yes, there's something to that. Adnan, prophet on his rock – perhaps he should have been left, and not been posed those Stella questions. Running errands, hiding the mature bananas under the presentable ones. I wrap the globe – Sophie's gift – and leave it in a pile, to sell as grapefruit.

Sophie says, 'I feel responsible for you. I hate it – it makes you so dependent.'

'Don't be so Dutch,' I say.

'But I am Dutch,' she says. 'Maybe another of my friends – she can instruct you more.'

This is my type. She smells of aquavit – yes, she's grubby, too. Wanda – maybe 'the wan', the wanderer – she says, 'Your journey – leave them alone, those guys. They want survival, just like people here. They fight it out – your quest, it doesn't change a thing.'

'There has to be a big idea, the problems likewise – some solutions,' and I gaze expectantly, sincere, though unconvinced.

She twists about, some itch, bone-deep: she makes a funnel of an ear, she says, 'I hate this song, don't you? It's music from the monkey-pit.' She sings along. '"Livin' in the state of dreamin'...."'

I say, 'I hadn't thought. It's all like that. These songs are brief.' She sways. I say, 'How'd I get out of it, this quest?'

'There's no way out,' she says. 'Some cells have locks. The music goes on day and night, it changes, but you can't get out.'

'Maybe,' I say, despairing, 'we could do a stretch together...' and she interrupts, 'No, no, just leave that be. I'll not come with you, my lad. I want to sit here in the park, drink vodka, maybe some sex, over in those bushes there.'

We drink together, then she says, 'Tear them down, tear them all down ...Those statues, gods with trunks and tusks – they're ugly things. The Colosseum – ugh! A pile of bloody stones. Those ruins all – let's pull them down, and make them ruins, then we'll build some more, those too – we'll make fine ruins from them, and take the stones, and pile them up and drink and dance upon them all ... Civilisation – those guys have got it right – it's in the head – tear down the stuff, the things, the tombs. Read those old Krauts – they knew it best, that beauty's in the head, the rest is vanity, display. Gold. Paper. Promises. And debts.'

I say, quite desperately, 'I can't dissent – but, it isn't beauty in the head, it's gods they want. It's worse: a statue, you can give it milk, and leave. But when you've gods, stuck in your head, it wears you down, it's like a swarm of flying things that build a nest – they block your eyes, they buzz all night, so's you can't sleep.'

'So what?' she says, 'and if you're right?'

'Well,' Sophie says, 'has that fixed everything?'

'I heard it all before, and many times. Destroy the ruins, then build more and knock them down. It's quite a cult. But – I'm looking for the base, where Wanda, Stella get their start ...'

'Time you were off, at all events,' she says. Her hands that hold and push.

I wonder – which of the devils have I made the pact with? And how do Pedro, Adnan, spend the time together? – every evening, Pedro explains with wit and resignation how he has cheated and been done down, during the day. Commerce, is all. And Adnan nods. He never smiles.

Stella – that book she reads, the pages blank, and then long preparations for her lonely sleep.

There's Wanda – at the quarrelsome point, her two companions on the bench, two Poles, or Lithuanians. There comes Sophie, lump of food in foil, 'It's just for you,' she says to Wanda, disapprovingly all round. Wanda waits till Sophie turns, and tips it in the grass. Wanda's on the express route. The aquavit goes down and down.

Stella said, 'Your journey is the history of the human spirit.' Or did she say, just 'part' of it. And add, 'no destination, and no starting point.'

She has no place that she can leave.

Yes, at last I'm leaving. And – oh no, here's Pedro. 'You can't investigate me if I'm not around,' he says. He takes my arm, it hurts – and soon we're flying through the air. 'Down there,' he points to brown corrugations far below, 'they kill you for the opinions that you hold, while where we came from,' and he cranes around, 'they say they kill you for your actions, and they're indifferent to what you think. The highest value there's indifference, it seems,' he cackles, asks for lots of drinks, and cushions too, says, 'I always try to memorise a thousand lines of verse on these long journeys – some epic, that is useful when you need to entertain in bus or train.' It seems to me he sleeps. Adnan will mind the stall.

Here we are. I say, 'Pedro, I'll always fly with you. You're by far the speediest.'

He's pleased. He says, 'Remember, the sun is always at your back,' and so it is: he goes on, 'That way the cinema can save your life. I saw it there – you beat your rival on the draw. He stares – there is no you. It is the sun. Creation, and a bullet in the eye, is what he gets. It's quite poetic, sends you on wherever's next, with revelation.'

The streets are dark, and up above, in sunlight, there's the upper floors – of banks, I guess, and similar. 'Never mind those,' says Pedro, pushing me down some slimy steps, 'You'd never find a crime in all that paperwork. Trust me, the Galileo axle ...'

There's serious guys, losing their cash, and ladies in those bowler hats. A host of flies, of course. There's chickens being plucked, guitars too. Pedro says, 'Whoa – don't use the pintables, they'll go Tilt!' and so they do. 'We're on the wheel,' and so he concentrates, the wheel spins like a coin, it tilts and tilts, and down it comes, the silver bullet lodges in our slot. 'We've won, we've won,' says Pedro. 'That's when you use the Galileo axle right.'

We don't trust it here, there's silver bullets all around, some are in guns; we cannot see the sun if it is at our backs.

'I take the hits,' says Pedro. 'You're a butterfly, you can't.'

There's bustling music everywhere. 'Open the kingdom,' it says, and sets you tapping.

Pedro says. 'The song – it's by a Yankee. Somewhat kitsch, but none the worse for that. It's just a song – no kingdom opens,' and I say,

'I like it here. And I want to see the shacks, the huts, to get the picture whole.'

'Of course you would,' laughs Pedro. 'You wouldn't recognise an evil thing if it bit you on the thumb. Now we've financed our trip – open the kingdom! Off we go. This is the civil part. They don't shoot here until they lose.'

I say, 'Pedro, you're just cynical. Besides, the networks – they're beyond the good, the evil,' and he hugs me, he's quite lovable.

'My dear,' he says. 'Crime, punishment – what I can't stand, is if it's done gratuitously. Crime is quite a human thing, and understandable, everyone wants survival. And – punishment. Well, that will come – from someone, even me – the pilferers, slit-purses, cut-throats, they all know what life will bring. Fight hard – and take the consequences. The problem is,' and he points to guys against the walls, their ponchos drawn up to their hats, their faces far away, 'the ones who can't do anything ...'

I interrupt. 'Here –' we've come to where there's shacks, and guys whose ears are tuned to turning earth '– there's nothing to be done, it seems.'

'You've surely not a feeling against capitalism?' he asks, offended, 'It is the central pillar of my thought, my world view hangs on it. What better way to set up crime and punishment, and saints and shrines?'

We squat inside the oven that these guys are living in, there's flies, although their nourishment is scarce. Pedro says, 'At this point, we consider rescuing. Of course, we could not organise a rescuing for everyone in stasis, danger, or accidie. To fly them round, and find them jobs – imagine, it's not feasible.'

He stares at me, quite troubled. It's hard to know how to respond. 'Of course,' he says, 'bad is bad. It's worse if you know better, and you needn't do it. Anyway, I can't enforce –

like you, I judge.' He laughs – peeks into one of the oven dwellings they use here, and laughs again, 'No, you're not there. Just my small joke, about your bones. You see – it's dates and figs. That is my network. Those are global foods, they're all you need. I'm wholesale, just like Adnan. And I often ask myself, "Rescue – is it the best? Was it by chance?" You, a rescued guy, a refugee – you're in a different category, you're in-between. You flee the bad, with no hope for the good.'

He seems to regret this, his expansiveness: he says, 'At any rate, there is no rescue here, for now. I have no method for it. Here,' and he hands me a rustling bag, 'Take these coca leaves, they're promised to the scaffolders. When we leave, we'll say it's khat, for our next stop. I've cousins on the force ... They love my figs and dates ...'

He's now unstoppable, he talks and talks, 'Ah Sophie – a person really good – not that it helps her, being quite insufferable. And Wanda now – that aquavit is painless till it's irreversible, and then! wow, she'll do a tarantella! All people seem to want to leave something. Wanda – she feels the pain, ours, hers, it's everywhere, she'll leave some, when it's time, that is for sure. A real good person, too. They're not anonymous, the dead. It's just they have one name – "the dead". It's hard, not to shed a tear – each wanting immortality so bad. Even those Americans up north – their gods have made them do some dreadful things – but still, I have to trade with bad, as well as good.'

While he talks, we wander round, like tourists, though he doesn't seem to see the sights – the pyramids, the skeletons, the skulls: I say, 'This place – it doesn't let you fool around, forget – the ending is the end.'

'That's true,' he says. 'That's maybe why we have to leave, before some bad thing happens ... if it hasn't done already ...' and I think of the family, their clay pot, crouched around, the rumble as the world goes on, turning and gyring. I say, 'There's lots that you could do ...' I think of marching, unions – and he's annoyed, 'Yes, yes, there is. But I'm not there to do it.'

He's calmer now: he says, 'I love Adnan's civility, his cultures, all that stuff. Of course, there's dialectics there, a lot of them, no doubt the civilisation will destroy itself – there's many ways. It's all a building site, it's hard to tell where knocking down becomes a building up. But still – our business is the figs and dates. Just need some handfuls, hope it rains, and you are set for centuries.'

'Of course,' says Pedro, 'you must seek the right. But what's the good, if you're not on the winning side?'

We're where he says he found Adnan. It's all too quiet, some things have been knocked down.

'You should stand here,' says Pedro, 'while I do my thing, and maybe put together winning sides that's also good.'

He scuttles off. There's no one at the windows here, there's lots of garbage ... high blocks, unwatered yuccas, someone's playing heavy metal, so faint it seems a dream of paradise. I think, *If I am asked, who do I say I'm for? Freedom, the right, the good?* It's true, my duty is to find an order, discovering what Pedro does. His dates and figs. Yet – he should have told me, which side am I on? The winning one, and that's for sure. I hope. And in this street – who's winning here?

He's back. 'Look at those flies!' he says. 'No rescues here – there's far too many desperate guys. Not one with a smile like

Adnan's. Guys here – they're waiting for a revelation. That makes it worth the fight. They may not know – they'll go to work in factories, poor things. Some will surely be condemned. Let's hope that suffering makes you good. Besides—' he cocks his head and listens to the little rhythms far away, like field mice weaving nests '—no one listens now to metal sounds.'

We're both uncertain what to do. 'You see,' says Pedro, 'I do what I've always done. The trade. You have to leave enough to guarantee things carry on. I can't get rid of harvests in a flash, a bang, just sell them off. You can't just do your job, and let the heavens fall ... It keeps on keeping on, guys take a chance, their hearts are young, their minds unsure. Their families ... ah well, Adnan knows about that. Interests: you can't ignore them, whether it's survival or your three percent. Though here,' he laughs, 'you don't collect your three per cent, but someone does, I'm sure.'

A guy comes out and says to me, 'Come in. It's dangerous outside.'

'Inside you go,' says Pedro. 'I'll sort things out.'

The guy is well-informed, persistent, says, 'No shrines, no saints. No tomb that's higher than a hand above the soil. Don't you agree?'

Well, certainly I might. There may be something more, there surely is. I say, 'I'm one of yours, thus far. God was the architect, they say – maybe a fifteen centimetre limit for the height ... a little low?' I go on, 'I know, a hand that's raised by us, the human ones, is tall enough, and when you're dead you're flat, of course ...' I try to ingratiate with him, and with the guys I hear that's in the other room as well, when Pedro rushes in, he says:

'Of course, you guys – God wants you to be free, obey, and to be good. Above all, good. Or else. And now – the profs that's found the secret of the universe, that you knew all along – ask them! They want you to be good, no less. Be free, they say, obey our proofs, our architecture ...'

Those guys – they don't let on, which is their side. We fail their test, and fail again, but Pedro's not at all put out.

He pulls my arms, my hair, my nose. 'Away, away,' he shouts. 'What are you doing, chattering here – tombs, God and particles. What do you know, what do these guys ... what if they know, or don't? And while we're at it, where's that sack of coca leaves I left with you?'

'I left it on a heap,' I say. 'It didn't seem appropriate. And if I'm caught ...'

'That's right and wrong,' he says. 'You'd suffer if you're caught, that's right – but wrong, because it's mine, and now you owe me.'

I think of Adnan, safe within his jewel, his diamond. Space: dense, self-sufficient – with no hands, no buzzing things, no tiny clods that cruise like flies. Just diamond. And no Pedro.

'Where did you go, when I was interrogated?' I ask.

'Oh, meddling, just meddling. I can't resist,' he says. 'Power struggles. You know what they're like. All the same. Dreams and demonstrations. Not your concern – how could it be? No one can be surprised where these things lead to. But anyway – I'm just a looker-on. No money – just my figs and dates, my dates and figs.'

*

We go back where we left: I say to Sophie – 'Pedro and Adnan, they kissed when they met, but not like lovers. Maybe they were lovers when they parted, and now they're not.'

This interests her, and she speculates. I say, 'You don't care about my journeys. You think I make things up.'

'That's what journeys are,' she says, 'A make-believe.'

'Well, there's something more,' I say.

'What? That you discovered nothing, won't make report to Toopip, won't get your documents?'

'Yes,' I say, 'that's it. At least, I didn't betray a friend.'

'He betrayed you,' says Sophie, 'all the time. From winning at roulette, to drugs. Galileo axles, indeed! And sides. Where Adnan fled from – there's a polyhedron of them, sides – you can bet, Pedro's on all of them.'

I say, 'I met those rigorous guys. You know, I love extremes – believing really hard things, and doing them, come hell or happiness. Making hatred bubble forth from purity.'

'But you're not serious for long,' she says. 'You're the one who does the awful deed, his comrades drop him, and he never understands – he's frippery, he's bogus crystal. They can't stand him.'

This needs chewing over. 'Something big is happening,' I say. 'I want to be a part, or close, not snapping pictures from the wings.'

'You've no opinions,' Sophie says. 'You have all of them, just sprinkled on. You're not a proper refugee – you ran before they caught you. Perhaps you were subversive – how could they know? Or care? Those places – everyone is full of bile, you can't arrest the lot.'

'Being in the right. That's what you must be. Or seek,' I say.

Sophie says, 'You just want documents. From a place that isn't yours and you despise. You'll never go to work – you think you're clever. You're dissatisfied – that's different things entirely.'

I ask, 'How's Wanda?'

Sophie says, 'She has her acolytes. She's frizzing out her hair and speaks with tongues. She hasn't far to go.'

I'm keen to see Wanda.

Wanda says, 'I'm sure about my future. Let's drink together, I'll peek into yours.'

'No, Wanda,' I say. 'I want a broader sweep. Maybe some country where the guys are doing well. How do they fill their time?'

'That doesn't take a sibyl,' Wanda says. 'They do bit jobs and shuffle stuff around.'

'It's how I thought,' I say. 'Sophie says, for humans, that's the best thing that there is. Lay down some kids, a plot of land, and die. That is prosperity, she says. The others have it worse.'

'Alas, my friend, that is the truth,' says Wanda. 'It's why the aquavit can help – it calls to prophesy, even sex. The revelation is – there is no revelation: – at least for me. I am the mouthpiece, not the will, the brain. The rest is as your Sophie says: you get your documents, you cast your vote. And that is it, the best there is.'

The Lithuanians have gathered near, the couple sing a song in many parts – it's wonderful, it's an illusion, that's for sure, it is a marvel of the aquavit. I say, 'That singing, I can't bear it. I hope it doesn't open up the doors, and summon up the learned dead!'

'No, no,' they say, 'it starts and finishes in aquavit. The bottle ends, and so do you. Then there's another bottle – and another you.'

They're fine fellows, loyal, and clumsy too. They're tired of asking guys for things, and now they are at rest; they minister to Wanda. This, until there's argument, is peace.

The trouble is – Wanda's a specialist. Experiments, done on herself. She seems quite ordinary, but she wants to go down deep, deep, to reassure – that for her at least, no revelation comes. Her life, drunk down. You see the sun through glass, a little skewed. It's a lesson she wants to pass to us as well. Who knows – that in the end, she can be wrong. Revelation: it may come. For sure, she's gone too far along to turn back now. It takes a courage, that. It's cowardice, of course. You need those two together, boldness, timidity. That can make you friends, admirers – even worshippers.

I take these thoughts to Stella, and she says, 'Of course, you don't have to be an oracle. Someone to speak through you, and you pass on advice. Don't be an intermediary – they're who do the dirtiest jobs. There's open systems, infinite, not populated. Logic, mathematics. You inherit nothing, you have nothing to pass on. No land, no mule, no garden with a key. No massacre you did, just being ordinary, not standing out. No loyalty. No Kameradschaft.'

I say, 'Stella, I can't follow you. Your ancestors did soldiering and massacres, and so did everyone's – and so you wander into mathematics? It doesn't follow, doesn't compensate.'

'That is the point,' she says.

'I guess that's so,' I say. 'Things stay as they were, they are.'

She stares at me as if I'm stuffed.

Pedro has a warehouse now.

The 'Gay Greengrocers' sign is near illegible, and now the sign says 'Forbidden Fruiterers'. Adnan is tossing mandrake roots and cucumbers aloft a pile. The flies are numerous.

Pedro is desperate. He says, 'I do them favours, and the guys pay off with vegetables. I've stock – and no one buys. They give, and no one takes. And Adnan stacks. Is it my business plan? My marketing?'

I'd hoped to get some work with him. 'The Galileo axle. Couldn't you try levering with that?' I ask.

'To me,' he says, 'it seems like cheating. Maybe another journey, discovering a corner unexplored – beneath the sea, perhaps, or up among the yaks. People will ski and dive most anywhere, you find some barmen, open a shack, and so your fortune's made ...'

'But, Pedro,' Adnan says, 'this is your honest part. You're not a merchant of this stuff. You're into other things ...'

'Yes, yes, you silly boy,' says Pedro, hustling him away. 'My expertise is dates and figs, that's true. This stuff will rot ...'

I say, 'You whip it into healthy froth, put it in cans. That's what they do. Your fortune's here, and it ferments without a curse or plea. This stuff will make you live two hundred years – you label it just so, and wait. You'll see!'

Pedro says, 'Insurance time...!' and leaves.

I say to Adnan, 'Forget these silly greenery names. You call it all "Eternal Life", the cans, the store. You'll see – they'll not resist.'

He contemplates. He says, 'Wow! Yes, that's marketing! You deserve a secret, for thinking that. Or half one, anyway.' He whispers in my ear, 'Pedro insures himself. It's a safe bet – he'll never die. But when he goes around the world – he is a bank! He's worth more than ten countries in a heap. And he's safe too, it's worth no one's while to kill him – if they did, the cash all comes to me. I like your smile,' he goes on, 'And if it ever comes about that we both die, Pedro and me – all will pass to you. And then you'll know the rest, the whole secret. What he does with cash he borrows on his worth. Don't worry – we shall never die. I knew it, when I sat upon that pile of stones, and there he was. My rescue. How he suffered in that place, those flies a stinging halo,' and he laughs, '"Eternal life" – yes, that is brilliant. No one has ever thought of that before. How strange!'

'"Eternal Life"?' laughs Pedro, 'yes, that'll do nicely. Genius. Who can resist? And the three of us can travel. The green stuff will wait till whenever we get back. And you,' he turns to me. 'When we travel, forget your girl friends. My! You've women all around! And yet you don't perpetuate yourself. No kids, despite it all. We have to be immortal, Adnan and I, we spit on families,' and they both laugh.

'I'm straight,' I say, apologising. 'The girls have fine qualities which I don't appreciate,' and Pedro interrupts, 'When we're on the road, no one tries to look after the others, and resent it. That's your Sophie gone, quite done for. No alcohol – that finishes Wanda off. No massacres, no maths – forget your Stella. As for being straight – in your case, it's been quite unavailing,' and they laugh again. He says, 'Each for himself, and all together – that's the deal. Eat good, if eat you must. Follow the signs and count kilometres. No chanting, and no blisters.'

He's hard, but makes you feel warm and wanted, part of the management. There may be gifts to come.

Pedro says, 'Usually, I pass myself as impresario, when we go on tour. I do it well – nostalgia, ambition, schlock – like that short Italian guy that's in the movies. That's showbiz. Now, we must be careful,' and he peers around, an opera villain. Adnan too, gazes at the movement round – I remember, for him, there's fullness everywhere, there is no emptiness, the space is full, the stars are filled with stardust, and I feel his hand in mine. 'Courage!' he says, 'Pedro has cousins in the force. In every one.'

I'm quite surprised – his gesture.

Pedro is short, and swarthy too, a beetle, well-coordinated those many arms and legs: tickets, drinks, a rug – he's ready for the flight. Brother to that short Italian, always in the cinema. I say, a bit embarrassed by Adnan, 'No singing – I can't stand that awful Greek, inventing music with his piece of string! The octave! That's a pit that's hard to climb up out. It's all maths, and seven into eight won't go ...'

Pedro ignores this and says, 'Of course, I can't make anyone do anything. I can't lend unless they ask.'

'With him, it's different,' Adnan says. He's let go my hand, that isn't done again. 'States loan, and dealers too. But Pedro doesn't want it back, the cash. He ties it round your neck. It's favours that he wants, and in the end, you give him something. Then – he is content. A bargain. Both parties keeping to their word.'

Most places – we can't go to them. The country with the Galileo axle – 'No, too dangerous and dull,' says Pedro, 'and of course, Adnan's place is out.'

I think of Sophie, wonder who she's with. And Wanda ... dead? Transfigured ... Pedro says,

'No, no, my dear, it's not the time to think of loves not loved. And Stella too – you know,' and he whispers, 'Family troubles. Have iced her up,' and he looks solemn, and then breaks a grin, yes, like the little Italian guy who's always in those films.

We enter a country through a slit. It's rose quartz – 'Designed it all myself,' says Pedro. Adnan whispers to me, 'Pedro loves me, because I followed him. Guys do anything for cash. I do the job: the money doesn't interest. And if he goes ...' We're climbing up a mound – a hill that's made of broken amphora, a distant crowing, a polluted sky. 'There's folks around all right,' says Pedro, leaning with the slope. 'He doesn't love you,' Adnan whispers. 'He just thinks you're odd. I'm sorry, that you've lost your friends ...'

I say, 'I haven't. And it doesn't matter.' That's all schlock, like Pedro said. I'm carrying this five metre tube, the clay device for listening to the turning world. 'I always give the help distinctive burdens,' Pedro says. 'That way I see them from far off.'

'Aha!' shouts Pedro, waving a key. 'There it is at last.' A white stretch limousine. It's ours. The clay pipe fits in easily, of course. There's three compartments, Adnan takes the last, and Pedro sits atop three cushions, twirls the wheel. My little room ... some decent pictures – isn't that an amber wall? – and goatskin rugs. There's aquavit and choice of schnapps. Pedro and I – already we're quite drunk. The track is rough, the limo arches like a caterpillar – 'Whoa, me beauty!' Pedro shouts, and Adnan sleeps, I laugh.

'This is the life,' says Pedro. 'This makes sense of everything. Heaven and hell – what more could you want, and in the end it's all your fault. It is what everyone has asked about, and now you know ...'

Here come the billboards. 'Put up some of ours!' shouts Pedro. 'Here, they need Eternal Life. It hides those shacks.'

We shout down little telephones. 'If I were you,' I say, 'you need to sell the name quite quick, and dump your stock,' and Pedro says, 'It's froth, dear boy, some in our heads, and some in cans. It's vanity, all vanity!'

The other vehicles we see – they're all white stretch limos, windows painted black, and up and down the avenues we go, the lights are green, roads join us and depart without a salutation. Pedro shouts, 'Heaven and hell – it's all these people need. Who messed it up? I wonder. What more certainty can be required, for doing good or bad? You hate the octave – for me, it's the hypothesis, left dangling in some unsure future, that there may not even be. "If ... then" – there is no then, my friend – the then that's past is irretrievable, the mathematical then – it cannot come, it's paper tigers round the nursery walls ... The hypothetical if: well, if you don't know, can't see ... then "if" is anything at all, it's nothing ...' on he shouts.

'Pedro,' I shout. 'There's lots of buildings here, and limousines that glide like paper swans. But – there's no people visible. Publicity and aerials – lots: but ears to hear, wallets to pay – there's not a sign.'

It's rectilinear. I say, 'This is a China, then.'

Pedro says, 'It's one of them. I colour-coded all the gates. The next one is chalcedony, I think. And ours was pink. And, by the way – don't think of joining Adnan's plots. He isn't capable, it's harder than you can imagine, and you would do the dirty work.'

'I can't think what you mean, my friend,' I say. Then Adnan wakes. He shouts, 'Look! All those cinemas. All playing *East of Eden*. Now, there's a boy you'd want to die for. But it turned out differently. Our kind of movie, though. Deep, deep.'

'I'm looking for a guy ...' says Pedro: 'There he is!' Far far away, a slender man, white shirt.

'What does he want?' I ask.

'You note the lack of people here,' says Pedro. 'Maybe he will want to buy some in. A million. Say. It costs. They work for him, and for themselves. Of course, they're better off, or else I wouldn't fund the scheme. Besides, the life before – having kids and tending yaks, and going dirty – who'd want that?'

It's hard not to agree. He says, 'Or he might want to do some swank – look at those castles, on the ridge.' Indeed, it could be Scotland – there's a dozen, all with battlements, each one grander than the last ... There's stags that's rutting in the grounds, tied up of course. 'Now, that is class!' says Pedro. 'And more would still be too much.'

'These immortal projects,' Adnan says, 'they just make me cry. Tall buildings – never tall enough.'

The guy gets in. White limousines drive by. More flies get in our automobile, and some depart. They fly around, quite inconclusively.

Pedro drives ever faster. There's people with baskets on their backs, up and down the hills, like turtles – mountains spindly, like sweet potatoes, or like sages, tall bald heads, a sprout of trees on top.

'Look, Adnan,' says Pedro, turning round and spinning the steering. He can't see Adnan, of course. 'Look at all those pandas, waving. Look!'

'They're not real,' sulks Adnan, through the speakers.

'Sure, Adnan, they're real – they're just not real pandas,' Pedro says, as if we need a joke.

Cities flash by, and suburbs guarded: there's guys in black with guns, a Petit Trianon, a Sans Souci, and towers, all empty ... Trees unwatered, gas stations shuttered up, and limousines go up and down, and here's a dam, like half a bowl of steel, with little spouts of foam below – we shouldn't drive around the rim, but Pedro's shouting now – 'Adnan, you see! When you were rescued, that was no altruism, no attraction, no humanism, just a favour, that you must pay back. And yet – you plot! Against me! You cretin,' and he weeps, the car is bucking now, our tiny rooms rebound, the long clay probe is broken – now we'll never know how fast the world is turning, 'Oh yes,' Pedro screams. 'It's turning fast and faster, you can bet. When rescues don't go well, the only exit is a death ...' and Adnan, breathless, cries, 'Pedro, I loved you so – but then it ended , and it wasn't right that you should keep the cash, the power, and have it till you died – you know, it never would have passed to me, for you're immortal. I am not, the story runs and runs, and always you narrate ...'

On, on they argue, and the car breaks up – the dapper guy in front tells Pedro, 'Thanks – I'll settle for the castle now,' and out he drops, and Pedro shouts back, 'It's a deal, I'll mail the paperwork ...' and then we hit. Some rock. Two bodies – down the steep side, the dam – they glance the surface just the once, and bounce into the foam. 'Oh no!' I shout, 'no, no, it's Pedro,' and my amber wall cracks, shatters round, a shower of toffees –

I grab the schnapps, but for sure, my journey's over, and I shout again, 'Oh no, it's Adnan too!'

It's tragedy, the pillars of my world have cracked, down comes the tympanum ... I take a drink, and then – ah yes, of course, we're in China, one of those bodies must be made of straw.

Then Pedro leans in, he takes a drink of schnapps. 'My, that was tough,' he says. 'I can't abide a plot. Adnan, the silly boy – I told you he lacked expertise in things you need to know, like doing down the boss. And after all,' he turns to me – is that a grin? – 'conspiring, that is pretty bad.'

We tip the broken limo down – how satisfying, to see the bounce. 'That is too bad, about the transport,' Pedro says. 'I'll charge it to that guy's account, and send some porcupines, a gift to make it right with him ... Sugar him up. You see,' he turns from squinting out the carcass far below, 'you must be ready – "don't know, and don't remember", they're the words you use. They cover all your sins, omissions, wayward thoughts.'

We're waiting for a ride, and sit cross-legged by the road. An ancient sage comes up: he joins us, says, 'I must confess, that *East of Eden* isn't one I've seen, and now it's playing over town. I'll sit with you, and add my hope to yours,' and Pedro says. 'It's true, without a vision of that film, you're not a proper sage. But – hmmm – maybe it's better if you can imagine it, the drift, the lovely boy ...'

'No, no,' the sage says, much put out, 'one image isn't worth another. In my head and on the screen – they're different things,' and Pedro says that's not what most sages think, and there is silence for a while. 'The trouble is,' the sage pipes up, 'things have got broken – we can't hear the rumble of the turning world. And when things are set to rights – they all seem very like things were before.'

'I never heard such crap,' says Pedro angrily. 'Think scale, think big. Ambition. See, all these guys, who'd never anything but tending yaks – look what there's ready, waiting for them. Just walking into it...' and that is true.

The sage is quite abashed, he says, 'Well, sages never see the details like you do, you men of commerce, capital, and all the rest.'

We sit in silence, each one disappointed with who's next to them. I think – poor Adnan, hustled out, into his void, his space, his diamond.

Pedro says to me, 'Now you've Adnan's job, forget the nonsense of my immortality – that was a pleasantry between us, him and me, in cosy days. Remember only – the worst thing's being bad when you don't need to be. The guys round here, they need the cash. You must be generous. Also careful, even finicky. Suspicious too. You mustn't think, because a guy's a sage, he's trading wisdom. As for Adnan, well, when lovers cloy, and start to calculate, you should let go and forget ... sometimes an accident can seem just punishment ...'

We see the silver streaks, down the dam wall, that's where the car wreck touched. It didn't dent the steel. Some guys with banners pass along the road. They sing, 'No blood without a revolution'.

A limousine slows down, we hitch a ride. It's over, the adventure, and the business has been done.

I say, 'Look, Pedro, I'm not sure I want the job. Being lieutenant to you, being like that Toopip guy – it's not my scene.'

'You're chosen,' says Pedro. 'It's too bad. No scruple.'

'Look, Pedro,' I say. 'I'm not loyal. With you, being loyal's the first duty. Until death.'

'Yes, that's true,' he says. 'Hmmm. Disloyal. You can't mean to tell about the accident? My straw replica? Who'd you tell? It sounds far-fetched. We came in through the quartz – there is no paper trail ... But disloyalty can be got around – especially since you've no power to damage me.'

'No, no,' I say. 'I'm disloyal to everyone. Just as it comes. Whoever does the bad, the good – I'm quite indifferent.'

'Hmmm,' says Pedro. 'Maybe we should have accompanied that sage to *East of Eden*. You're a desperate case.'

'I love those that love me,' I tell Pedro, 'but when I stop – there is no pact.'

'Of course there's pacts,' he shouts, 'and treaties, contracts too. That's what sustains the world.'

'No, Pedro,' I say. 'It's the Galileo axle.'

Back home. I tell them, 'Adnan? He stayed there.' They're satisfied.

'Of course,' says Pedro. 'I just do the cash, just prime their pump. As for the things that people sweat about, that don't depend on cash – the justice, revenge, prejudice, spite – one day our brains will grow and sort those out. We're lumbered with what we started with – those brains, they need a refit, that's for sure.'

The warehouse is empty, except for hosts of flies.

'I sold the name, "Eternal Life", for lots. Some tobacco corp, I think,' he says. 'So you don't need to manage anything, just travel round with me.'

'Pedro,' I say, 'the straw man. Why two cadavers? What's the point of carting replicas around?'

'Oh,' he says, embarrassed. 'Just my old ritual. If your body's not identified, you're free to roam the earth. They never know me, or the other guy.'

I'm not convinced. I go to see how Wanda is. Her tiny flame is guttering.

'I told you, Wanda,' I say, 'nothing happens at the end, except the end.'

She says, 'I went as deep as deep, I flew, I sang, I screamed. I hit guys with the bottles, peed on our bench, and on myself. I went as far as anyone, until I can't return – I'll do a final dance, and leave my body to the crows. I suffered for you all ...'

'She did, she did, oh yes, she did,' the Lithuanians make a chorus of it, leaning on their staves.

'All on my own,' croons Wanda. 'I did it on my own.'

The Lithuanians – or Poles – her pilot fish, already they look round for some big fresh monster of the sea to dance around, and titivate. 'A bad end, like the seas themselves,' they say: 'All full of crap.'

Pedro says, 'Wanda won't get the respect that she deserves. A good, indeed a noble, person. Just – an idiot.' He broods, he says to me, 'It's hard to love me, that I know. But – I keep bargains. Even an accident foreseen, is part of keeping to the word.'

I feel uncertain: 'You'd the right to expect some loyalty,' I say.

'Oh, how I miss Adnan,' says Pedro, turning to me, 'and you are not the same.'

'I know,' I say. 'Adnan told me what you thought of me.'

Pedro ignores this. 'And now, the talk's about the end, not of Wanda, but the world.'

'I know that too,' I say.

'Who says?' asks Pedro. 'To me, we're near the start of things – at most, we're somewhere in between.'

'You know who says we're near the end,' I say.

'If all goes well, the population grows, there'll just be standing room for us,' says Pedro, irritably. 'If not, we shall end lying, stacked up on one another. Then, what's to become of me?'

The Wake

'Yes, yes,' cries Stella. 'We'll have a wake for Wanda. Even those Lithuanians – but only to sing.'

'She's not dead,' says Sophie.

'No matter,' says Pedro, 'I'll take her flame, and it'll light the banknotes that send her on her way. Then we'll take our trip,' he says to me.

'First, let me take you on a trip,' says Stella, enthused. 'To a lemma, far away.'

And so she does – we start with letters, figures. I recognise them all. It's easy to negotiate. I think of us, imagine, riding in an old Dodge truck, springs elastic, up the mountain – I say, 'Hey, those slides and sines, things invented – the trucks with logs, sliding down, the asphalt ends, we're climbing, wow, it's hot, the goats – now, mind the goats ...'

'The goat is you,' shouts Stella. 'Use your imagination!' – and I do, but, no, those systems, they're too much. A lemma – it's like a thumb without a hand. 'It's beautiful,' says Stella, and the others nod. They lie on it, horizontal, and watch the sky, inspired and fired.

'Yes,' says Sophie. 'Mathematics is the best. That is true humanism. No one falls off, no one tweaks their friend. No one gets stoned, or locked away for centuries.'

Pedro lies there, and he smiles: he says to me – 'Relax! Your trouble is, you jumped before they pushed. You escaped, so I can't rescue you. You're quite a drag – that's why lying on this lemma, you just want to run. It won't hurt you. Let it enfold...'

I think, 'Poor Wanda.'

'I'll do the eats,' says Sophie. 'And there's aquavit, of course. There's toffees too.'

They're the bits of amber, from the limousines. Some filled with human bones.

'Stella's thick,' says Pedro to me quietly. 'But her maths beats your old Dodge truck.'

'Hey guys!' shouts Sophie. 'We need a corpse, if it's to be a good wake. And Wanda can't be disturbed.'

Of course not. She must have reached the plain that slopes down, so you can't see the drop...

'Wait, I've an idea,' says Pedro. 'In my trunk ... And after, we'll set light to it, like the Vikings did.'

He lays out the cadaver. It is me. I ask, 'Pedro, where'd you get my pants?'

'Oh,' he says, 'it's just coincidence. One straw guy looks very like the next.'

Sophie and Stella are dancing like goats with the Lithuanians. They look like all other dancers. Is it sex or invocation? It's anonymity – if it's what eternity is like for humans, I don't enjoy it.

Pedro pulls me down to his mouth. 'Don't you ever think of all those other guys? The ones back home, where you got caught, and you were thinking of cucumbers, and they were on the rack, or on the burning bed, or under the waterfall, or being the light bulb, or having the finger-cracker?' He goes on.

'Yes, of course,' I say, 'all the time. It doesn't add up to anything.'

'No,' he says, 'you're the lemma here.'

'*Down in the amber mine*,' the Lithuanians sing loudly, '*I hid away me and mine – / They looked and found. Now we're seaward bound ...*'

'Let's snap ourselves out of this,' laughs Pedro. 'Of course, all the past has a terrible reputation, it's where so many things finished.'

We're all drunk. Only Wanda's probably not.

I say to Pedro, 'I thought lemmas were the starting place,' and he replies, 'You dummy – they're a high meadow – when your truck breaks down, you roll upon the grass, and stare up in the sun. That's a lemma. It's the end. Four-fingered glove.'

Stella hugs me – now she's dancing – over me, against me. My, she's powerful. 'Mmmm, yumyum,' she says. 'I could hug you till you squeak – you're like that Petroushka, a doll, a stallion. Just right for my bed!'

Now, here comes Sophie, and she's pounding Stella round the head – 'You primitive!' she shouts. 'You snitch! You snatch! Coplover! Corrupter of corruption, tormenter of the idle, waker of the dead! Leave my love alone!' And on she goes – it is humiliating, though it feels good to have protection.

'Leave me be!' I shout. 'None of you! You smother me, you goddam crocodiles, you drag me down, into the swamp: you

Liliths' – and at that they all pull back, and Pedro says, 'Poor guy. It is his past. He raves, and nonsense words come out.'

I say, 'Pedro, I want a side to be on. I need it – I know the bad people, they are infinite, spectral, they throng, they chatter. Being under them – it hurts. But – no humanism either – I don't want to be with guys because they're guys, good, bad, quite indiscriminately.'

He cocks his head, looks quizzical.

'Sophie and Stella – they survive,' says Pedro. 'And you don't. At least, you don't try. You spit in Sophie's soup – that's quite too bad.'

'Pedro,' I say, 'you're so like that small Italian guy, the one in movies. Don something?'

'No, no,' he says. 'Mafia? That's someone else entirely. I know who you mean, they all say that I'm like. Italians. Colonised by ghosts, that's them. White masks, white faces. Don't know who to get their independence from. So, that's not me. I'm independent, that's for sure. And as for names – I come across them all the time – they're just figs and dates. Names don't mean a thing, unless you have the person too.'

Stella and Sophie – they've gone beyond my sight. Maybe they embrace. I should too, I know. Instead, I go to Wanda, on her bench. Her eyes are like two mushroom caps – a circle of brown gills, two beige pupils where the stalk once was.

'I thought I'd like to be with you,' I say. 'And that it could be quite reciprocal.'

'Well, you can't,' she says. 'What you think – you can come with me, that I care? Fuck off,' and so I do.

The wake is quieter now, the Lithuanians are quarrelling – *en sourdine*, they say.

'I want to have my kids with you, Stella,' Sophie says, 'and not with him,' she points vaguely at us all, the rest.

'Come away, come away now,' says Pedro. '*Luxe, calme et volupté*. That's what's on my menu now. Look, we'll take this,' and he points to a Valiant, parked below. 'You get in anywhere with these. You don't need relatives who're on the force. These old cars touch the heart of every cop, they let you in to any country. You need never stop.'

'I should say goodbye,' I say. 'Start a relationship. There's talk of families,' and Pedro says. 'Don't illude yourself. Forget Wanda. Learning to forget – it is a principle.'

'We need to watch them burn the body,' I tell him.

'Well, since it's yours,' he says. 'But quick. All was an error; Adnan, the greenstuff. On the road!'

'That was your enterprise,' I say. 'Fruit. Not to be downplayed.'

'It's nothing,' Pedro says. 'Stella and Sophie now – they'll start a shelter, a workshop, for guys like you, for wanderers who flee before you have the bad thing done to you. Those guys – they'll all be put to mending electronic stuff. Those little nimble fingers! It's genius, those women. Too bad they didn't invent capitalism, they'd have made it work. Now, charity and sweated labour, that's their business model – under the counter, too.'

I don't look in the trunk. I drive, and Pedro's in behind, reclining. 'Faster, faster! Onward, onward,' he shouts. 'Childe Roland, let's hear you toot your mighty klaxon!'

There's Wanda's patch of green. She waves, or maybe it's a spasm, lifts a veiny arm, a mast with ropes, blue ropes, around. A schooner going down. She cries, 'Away, you dreary Dutchmen ...' and the Lithuanians sing on.

'Why does she think we're Dutch?' asks Pedro. 'We are anything but ...'

'Sophie's Dutch,' I say. 'That's Wanda's little beacon, nationality, on her globe,' and I remember Sophie's globe I threw away, among the figs and dates and flies.

'Forget all that,' says Pedro. 'Just go fast. We leave all this for good.'

Maybe I'll find his second secret – must be how the credit, the first secret, turns to notes and coin.

'Forget about secrets,' Pedro says. 'Open the windows, hope the flies get sucked away. My! Those burning olive trees – the people need a revolution here, for sure. That French guy – had it right. I'm glad I stuck to figs and dates, and let the olives be. People take revenge on them, those trees, they last so long, so rich, and so benevolent.'

We drive fast, so fast I'm scared. We don't seem to hit things. 'That's right, always faster,' Pedro says.

'Maybe we should stop and pray,' I say.

'No, no,' says Pedro. 'Guys here would steal our shoes.' He hands me something, though my hands stick to the wheel, 'Eat, eat,' he says. 'These baklavas – they do us for cash.' There's a box of them – 'The best I ever ate,' I tell him, and he says, 'They make you sick, but don't refuse ...'

We fill the car with ancient fuel, that guys with wolf-eyes bring in cans. 'I'll seem ungenerous,' says Pedro. 'But here there's people doing bad without the need of cash from me. And here, they're poor. I wouldn't think of going where they're rich – my little sweeteners, they don't attract when you've got loads of cash. I'm stressing quality now: a premium for your being loyal, and sticking to the pact. For all the others too, who'll do the same.'

I didn't make a pact. I drive, that's all. I think of Adnan. Did he have a pact?

Back there, there's Pedro, downing baklava, he eats and eats, we pass through countries big and small, and guys who're at the payback time, they make excuse or slink away, and Pedro writes their name.

'Just look at all these holy sites,' he says. 'No, don't stop, and don't slow down. They bear a jinx. You won't find any in New York, not one. It's good that here there's hope, despair – and there they've none.'

We drive faster and faster, 'fill 'er up' we say, she empties out.

Pedro says, 'Of course, it's sad that in the end there's punishment. Not by my own hand, of course, though in my name. But it's evident – most who take out loans, can't pay them back. You know from the beginning, that it's vanity. Some get punished too for nothing, nothing at all – that's to avoid a pattern, being too rigorous, too mathematical. It's not all carrots, not all figs and dates. In everything, there is a whiff of justice. That's the rule.' He points, 'Here we're at Adnan's rock. Justice was done to him. The loan redeemed.'

Ahead, we see a line of tanks. 'Overtake – you must get past – see how they chew up the road,' shouts Pedro.

'No room,' I say. 'Let's stop and sleep.'

'No sleep, no sleep,' he says. 'And can you ride a horse?'

'I never tried,' I say.

'Then overtake!' And so we do, by driving in the ditch and in the stony fields. When we've passed, we're out of gas, the tanks go by as we fill up – and so we start again.

'We're fortunate,' says Pedro. 'This road has no end – see, all the holy places, factories, the blocks where people live and reproduce, the shops where you can place a bet or buy a drink,' and on he goes.

'Is it a worldview that you're laying out?' I interrupt.

'Oh no,' he says. 'It's just my job. The thing that interests me's excess. The ordinary stuff – is this,' he waves round the scene. 'You might say, the fun is in apocalyptic things, the castles built, the countries bought, the visions hoisted into place. I make it happen, then I watch ... the dignity evaporate.'

He's got a hubble-bubble going in the back – I can't see out the screen for smoke. He says, 'Then let the flies lead on – you'll always find them, there before you, busy with their work. They find corruption, and eliminate its trace. They'll always beat you to it, and a rearguard stays when you have gone.'

He talks, he talks, 'Ah yes, the second secret. Poor Adnan – yet he had half a brain, and you have just a quirk. Death of the pope, a massive war – those are not secrets, those are certainties. The second secret – it is infinitely long. If only we could think – after the baklava, the nargileh, of something new that gives to man that sense of ease, of *luxe*, of *calme*, of *volupté* ...'

'So,' I say. 'It's just favours, knowing these wolf-eyed guys, and checking up. No politics. No sorting out. Now, if it was me ...'

'Whoa!' says Pedro. 'Remember Adnan! Stick to the easy life – lend and foreclose. Or else ...' and he gestures to look out the window, down, and it's true, there's an abyss, a road, a fortress. There's gliders up above. 'There,' says Pedro. 'They don't look for you. They know. They're not like hawks or eagles – they don't swoop. They crap upon your head. And there's your politics, blood on the road.'

He eats more baklava, then: 'I put an amber wall for you, when we were in the limo. You didn't even have to drive.'

I say, 'That amber, it was full of bones. The Poles, the Lithuanians – they'd seen it all before, the massacre ...'

There's night. At dawn, he says, 'Usually, you can fix most things with cash.'

'Pedro,' I say, 'you don't fix, you lead guys on, provoke.'

'Be very careful, what you say,' he says. 'Be very, very careful.'

'Oh,' I say, 'don't get me wrong. I like it – that provocation, it brings out the truth.'

'Oh,' he says, 'it's back to truth we are?'

I'm tired. I don't think that I could stand, get out the car.

Pedro presses on: 'I never fail, you know, though all the loans are bad, the pacts banal. How? That's the secret of the secret. But, my lad,' and he pokes me with something sticky, in the neck, 'you've hidden lots, confused things too. Those women were more enterprising.'

I say, 'Maybe I took the wrong path. Forgot things. Like, we broke the pipe, for listening to the axle.'

'Chance and necessity,' says Padro briskly. 'You didn't believe, not in any of this, the faith lost or melting, the beauty gone, temptation fading too ...'

'Of course not,' I say. 'How could I, or anyone?'

'We have a pact,' he says, 'of sorts.'

'No,' I say. 'I'm with you for convenience.'

Pedro laughs. 'You're nothing, and it suits you. I've showed you how it works, everything – it leaves you quite indifferent.'

'If I had stayed, back there, home country, and they had worked me over, bad, me knowing all of them, quite intimately – was that a choice, more solid, more authentic than driving you, and spinning down your route? Is that your point?' I ask. 'Or is it our convenience?'

'Yes, maybe, no,' says Pedro irritably. 'I know my rules, not yours.'

'Pedro, you're the wrong side for me,' I say. 'It's nothing about you, I suppose – it's that I can't do something else. But something else is what I want to do.'

'I'm only figs and dates, my dear,' he says, seeming hurt.

'Maybe it's the flies, then,' I say. 'They're in the baklava.' And so they are.

We stop quite often now. We both get out the car, and watch the camps, the campfires, sometimes a person with a flute, that doodling chant, the cities all lit up, deserted by night, waiting for aliens ...

'Get out the car! At once, get out the car,' says Pedro.

We stop, and I get out. It's dark, he's dark.

Oh no, must I box? Or wrestle?

'Your exploration of the human possibility is done,' he says, quite calm. 'It's inconclusive – that's your fault, and problem.' Then he shouts, 'The design, the design. You were blind to the design!'

Here, there's flowers of blue and red, of no-account, and what has been a trough for watering animals. I think, 'It's paradise abandoned,' and I smile. This place is where the guys wait to be picked up, go to some site, and dodge the boss and cops all day, and start again.

The flies are still asleep – there's some mosquitoes, though.

'You smirk,' says Pedro, 'since your sad life is spared. You've had it better, and you didn't want to know. Now you're wiser, so you can suffer more.'

I say, 'But Pedro, I was loyal and unambitious. Drove like a fiend. I served.'

'Exactly so,' he says. 'No rescue. This is pay-off time.'

He twists into the Valiant, and down he goes – he spins it, then he guns it straight. The tail-lights have gone out, he's gone too, faster than a bullet, raising dust. Always there will be someone to rescue, to take the wheel – you find them everywhere, they wait by similar troughs, the blooms are no-account.

If test there was, I have come through, not first or last, but live.

2 Landfall

Julie

We're a bunch of international spies, we make watch-lists on an island on a secret lake. Some of our suspects are really good guys, and some get tortured and killed in various ways.

'That button! It opens all the cages. No, no! Touch nothing!' I have to shout at her.

There's music everywhere, it could be Bruckner. I throw the headphones at her: she laughs and says, 'Enough, the noisy music. Look, I've brought you ...' from the cellophane, a disc – it plays, a violin, alone, sounding between sobs and chuckles, and the fiddler now vocalises along, with chirrups and slides. I say, 'It's skeletal,' at a loss.

'No, not bones – very thin meat,' she says.

I say, 'No one before has ever given me a disc I didn't like.' We laugh. I ask, 'Who d'you belong to? You're good, I see – the good ones come by helicopter. At the start, we are all good. The bad ones leave by ship.'

'I'm your friend's,' she says. 'Erik. If you can call us friends. And how do you like your awful job?'

'You have to feel some empathy,' I say. 'The suspect guys we list – lives at a chase's end, lives hunted, traumatised, corrupt, rich, poor, persecuted. Suborned. Some dedicated. But then – we can't expect to understand the thickness of the thing itself, the happenings, – bombs, bullets, manifestoes – or not. The being, not just doing. Then justice – that must be done in finite times. You have to trust the guys, our guys, so they call themselves, that make you sum it up, finger someone. And then, they punish.'

'My! Is it convinced you sound?' she asks. We laugh again. I say,

'Waiting for the bad guys – it's like watching back skin, waiting for a pustule. A plain with gopher holes, surely snouts pop up. Of course, that's what skin's for – to breed the warts and boils, the freckles, tumours, pushing up. The causes: what their ancestors ate, or midday suns. Who's is that body, anyway? Who's sick, who's natural? It's history, not boils.'

'It's hard to talk these things right out,' she says. I say,

'We don't say anything, not us, not on this island, in this lake. I see the names, I think – "maybe their desire will wilt, friends change, honour is vindicated or worn thin" – it's anger versus fear, both long remembered. Bad guys. They have soft fear, for all those mistakes you mustn't make: it drops as rain. Then hard fear, down come the rocks: vendettas, promises.'

'Or just punks.'

'Sure, lots of punks.'

We stare: the screen. A million names, suspected. If you find a reference, open a file on them. Directories of suspects. Off to the camps, or worse. Or nothing. Each name, with a symbol added, marks a potential. Some future is hypothesised. The fear of God is all around, in them, in us.

'It's not quite right for you,' she says. 'So many suspects. Numbers. It's hard to grapple with.'

'No, no, we don't do that, assessing,' I say. 'We file them by: inspiration of the left or right, the family, the clan, the crap idea, the truth, the power. The scholars and the sheep.'

'Julie tells me,' says my friend, Erik, the boss, 'something quite grave. That you've uncertainties, not doubts. Uncertainties is graver, graver much by far than doubts. The trouble is – your friends. You see them so. All over. Comrades – woven with the rest.'

'Who's Julie?' I ask. 'I thought she'd only come to screw.'

'She's my boss as well. My girl ...' It's clear – he thinks a while of Julie. Then, 'You have to leave the island, Jan. By ship.' He twists the music off my ears, listens, exclaims: 'Why! It's birdsong, and so loud, symphonic.'

On the lake there's icy storms. The ship – it smells the deep, down goes its nose, then up again, white like a slice of cake with icing. Hoses, the axes – ice, what a labour. The ship longs to go down, its airy belly brings it up, over and over. Each time, a boom, a drumbeat, the distant clang – something inside, or do we strike? – another ship, down there below, sunk, voyaging along? And so thin, the steel, the ship a wedge – 'not a destroyer, a frigate,' shipped in overland by train, a rusty kit. The matelots say it's a 'frig-it'. Destroyers – us, listing the lineages, the referents, the rules.

Here you can be a sailor in the dark – down below with the engines. Or in the white, the light on deck. A matelot says to me,

'All the black matter we can't see. Those atoms held together by things unknown – are these problems, stored up there, waiting to be solved? Or are they pits, the ends of paths without a destination? A proof we're right, or that we're wholly wrong? The things that never fit. Don't they worry you?' He grasps me, dangles me. Grey waves. And draws me back. His reddish frightened face: "No, not any more," I say.

Julie – a tall girl.

Those symbols by the files; millions of names, all threatening. At sea, the sickness is like pregnancy with a beast unbearable. I was not much seasick. I chose to help on deck. Quickly we love the ship. The sea, its birds. The captain, fighting in many wars, so strict, a coward, furled in his bunk. Far off, the little lights, the railhead, the trains pulled round by night. Each wave a pit, a clang. Home to the cold fish, brother to the *omul'* that only lives in Lake Baikal. Now, a shore line with nomads. The captain pleased to see us go. We dance along the quay, our legs would plunge again, into the troughs.

Life – mostly it's about spying: guys in huts, and guys in tents, guys in caves. Lives in archives, talking on the phone – you'd want to hide, mostly, throw every trace away. I spy, they all spy, with little fingers, little eyes.

Here's the store – what big boots the nomads have ... Here the empty boxes smelling of clean old days: Sunlight, Persil. Chocolate and cocoa. A history there, of slaves. Buy vodka, lots of it, more than I can carry. They all stare, the nomads, not like in the movies, where they dance and smile.

I reason with myself. I left – they fired me – although I found it easy to judge actions. Where I stumbled – was intentions. Intentions and consequences – those are the slippery things. The bad guys who act – that isn't hard to judge ... It's all the rest ...

And then I think – I wasn't called upon to judge. That was for others. Maybe that was what was irksome, never to conclude. Yet if you judge, they say you must feel sympathy – and yet, my task excluded sympathy, though if you felt for someone, even a punk, an opportunist, maybe you closed an eye or two ...

'That is still judgement: that, you weren't called upon to do.' Again, it's that matelot, the chatter about black matter that we cannot see – and yet, for sure we see it, like the black cats in the black. Their yellow eyes. He buys some vodka, more than he can carry. Always the voyage to the island with the ship empty, then it takes the bad guys out, away from our island in the lake. Those guys, the experts – Russians, Yanks, all sorts. Castled in the silos, yellow like marzipan, tiny windows – black currants.

I book into the Grand Hotel. Then Julie calls me. Julie, a nordic type, white skin, red lips, my boss's girl, herself a bigger boss. So what.

She says, 'I think of you, of you always. Remember, how I saved you, from that awful job. How can you navigate – those intents, those wills, the guys that will to right and left, to death and life, and heaven too, no doubt? Those lists, and at the end – the camps? Or executions, forced enrolments?'

'Well, Julie,' I start off, 'you know, it wasn't easy – all the other guys, they took me for some patsy, a philosopher. Just wanting more than I was asked to do, and never doing it, not knowing what I hadn't done ... Then bad guys, turned out good guys, then, they were my friends, companions.'

'Yes, yes,' she says, 'I know all that. You're quite unsuitable.'

There is a silence. Then she says, 'I love you. Could you love me?' and she puts a pause between the two parts of the question. Two questions. Maybe a command. Of course, I say,

'Yes, yes, Julie, of course, to love you's more than easy, it's the natural thing. And more – it's human, absolutely human ...' I'm enchanted, now I must convince myself still more and deep. We should see each other, sort it out. I'm quite enthused. Why not?

She drives up to the Grand Hotel. I've my decision, and I hug her, I embrace her. This is happiness indeed. She says,

'Well, that's decided then. I knew it was the best for you – for me, of course. And tell me, how can you afford a Grand Hotel?'

I say, 'The carpets – see, they've all been cut down, they come from even Grander parts. As you go up the stairs, higher and higher, you see where all the frays have finished up.'

'Well, that's another mystery resolved,' she says, briskly, in a nordic way: 'And now – I have to leave. We'll surely be in touch. This is my happy day, you know,' and so I ask,

'Where to, and how long?'

'For sure, I have to work and move around. It's not so strange, you know. A job I like to keep. Just try to understand.'

We walk around the town, we're hand in hand. It's quite a modern place, no nomads, though there's horses still.

'Julie,' I say, 'I don't feel like hunting down my friends.'

'Goodness, Jan,' she says, 'I hope you're not a pain! Of course, we all have friends, we let them off our hook, and they do awful things, that's for the best, and history will judge. Our friends have friends and enemies as well, that's how it goes. It turns out for the best, most times – they do what they must do.

The thing I do, I watch you little guys, like you, you do your little job. You must not judge. Or let guys off. That's all.'

Sometimes now I help out, in the hotel kitchen.

'I can't love someone who always smells of fish. Fried, too,' says Julie.

'We all here smell of fish. A speciality of the lake.'

'Haha,' says Julie brightly. '"The higher up you go, you see the frays." And "all are fishy here" – you're quite a stylist!'

'That isn't quite the word,' I say. 'And Erik?'

'Oh,' she says, 'he's quite suitable, just now.'

Oh no – here's that goddam scientific matelot. 'The frigate sank,' he says. 'I have some fish.' And so he does. 'You see,' he insists, ignoring Julie. 'Black matter. That's what you investigate. A block upon your path. You have the idea that all progresses, that you can't be wrong. The same with those bad guys. Suppose that think and read – that is "invent", and "bang" is act. It all connects. One adds to one. So – if you don't start off, born from the rightness, and ancestors that's right as well – you end up bad, and in the cage.'

'Be quiet!' I say. 'I don't think that. That's why I'm here at frying time.'

He goes on filleting his gift.

'No, no,' I say. 'You only take the bones out for us. The others – they can do it for themselves. The ship – who was to blame?' He tells his tale:

'The tempest! Like the ghost ship, there we were, wallowing through the fantasy – the dead all round, the spirits, ghouls – it made you think of witches, of little buzzing things with voices dire, foretelling; rivets, maybe, that groan and pop. The deck turns vertical, the captain cries "Abandon, oh, abandon me, into the deep I slide." And so he did.'

'There's no way now to get the bad guys off the isle,' I say. 'They'll stay and fester there.'

'It's simple,' Julie says: 'All the bad guys are sailors. All the sailors are bad guys. If a bad guy isn't a sailor, they work in the kitchen. All the people in the hotel are bad guys. The captain is the worst of them. He's with the fish. The fish are in the kitchen – you cook; that matelot, Nestor, he guts. You see, life is really quite simple.'

The sailor says, 'When Old Whiskers, Stalin, was alive, they hid whole cities – this lake too. There is no map. It's bigger than Baikal. These fish – are like the *omul'*, but they're sweeter. And the lake is hidden still. It's policy. And now – without the ship, who knows what those guys will do, marooned out on the island?' And on his long smoked and salty face he puts a grin.

Julie ignores him, and she says to me, 'Power or freedom. Which do you prefer, my love?'

'Neither,' I say.

'Well, cook your fish then, silly boy,' she says affectionately. 'Anyway, there's lots of other presents you could have.'

'You should have chosen one of those she said,' the sailor says.

'Which?' I ask, amused. 'Which would you choose?' he says.

'Oh, power, no doubt. The choice is agony, of course. Either is a pain. But power, well, if it doesn't suit, you still have freedom, you can try it out.'

I say, to comfort, 'We still have our Intelligence. More chic than power or having fun. It's just routine.' They don't hook on to this, and Julie says, 'Of course, if we can't get bad guys out by ship, we can't get good guys in. I have a movie of the island guys, and what they're doing now, since I can't drop in on them. If you see things, they can seem more real.'

I think – that takes care of Erik, then I say, 'If you can't travel, Julie, you can come up to my room.'

She's disappointed at some thought – of being in confinement here, or coming up with me. She says, offhand, 'You pixel, Jan,' but up she comes.

It's like being with Norway. Sometimes it's green and warm. That's what I tell Nestor, the matelot.

We watch the tapes –

On the island, they are having fun – there's the captain, crawling up the shore, quite moribund. The good guys have a group, glam rock, it seems. There's Erik, top hat, frockcoat – 'he wears them well,' says Julie. There's snow around, but all are frolicking and glittering, we're lucky there's no sound, and some are dressed as sprites, and some as hairy beasts, ladies in wimples, mouthing Elizabethan jokes. We're quite aghast. 'Where's the Intelligence?' the sailor cries – 'How fortunate, that our hotel can't sink ...' forgetting he's a bad guy, like all us guys, and maybe Julie too.

Throughout the world, the battle's on. The good, the bad, it's like old plays of kings and kingdoms all made up and cast poetic, maybe add some witches round a pot. Julie's in tears – 'I can't go in, if there's no boat to ship the bad guys out. The group – they wear the clothes, the beat is absent, though.'

'They fight on everywhere,' Nestor says. 'In from the desert, capturing their old towns, their fortresses, once more. To you, it looks all sand. And snow. Those camel tracks of empires fallen in the wilderness. The rust. The dust!' he laughs, proud, amused with himself: 'Succession and secession, the best to oust the good, the bad is trailing there behind – no one's supposed to want it – how it lasts! The captains, moribund, come crawling up the beach – and then, they dance. See their top hats glint! Look, Julie – that is where there's beat, and fornication quite industrial. See them spring to life renewed – a verse, a poem, sets them off, see how their faces glisten with the paint, their beards jut out – no, not a *danse macabre*, a dance of death – Julie! It's life! Look! There goes the last fish, twisting out its ghost, maybe a curse – they gulp it down. There's nothing left, and on they dance, and sing, and call on gods and goodness. Would you have it otherwise, my dear? We must be there, still dancing, at the end, and round and round, and spit the bones in someone's hat, and on and on, and even when the end has come, we whirl and spin. And that is how it has to be, dear Julie! There is no other way. It is quite suitable,' and Julie says,

'Yes, yes! Quite adequate, to tasks that are at hand. Out with the incompetent, the ditherers and the patsies, the ho and hum. Just do it, do the job, and on it comes, and on and on.'

She's quite illuminated, maybe in her mind she's dancing on the shore, as Erik's party girl, and emperors restored, and mountains made of gold, and talking birds, and eating lean and having kids and keeping to the path.

She turns on us – 'I know! They've given up! Just having a good old-fashioned time. And I am not!' she screams suddenly. 'You don't make me happy, not you, not Nestor. Where are the answers? – as you creep around what you don't know – give me some hard, some quartzy stuff ...' and Nestor says,

'Well, if you want to know. Reason and science – they have screwed things up. All the stuff that we don't know, that we can't see, or hear or smell. The eighty-five per cent of blank and blot, that we know not,' and his eyes roll up, he rhymes, he is entranced – 'That's where you should start. Not leave it to the end. Error, dear Julie. That's the bog where we have ended up. A mass of things we've no idea about, no tools to dig and shift. We're at the end, my dears. It's ignorance, of everything. Just the indifferent, the trivial stuff, the lemmas and the arabesques – that's what we concentrated on – and they are dust, they're ash, a feather from a flighty bird.'

I'm at a loss: I ask, 'Who was the captain? He's the bad element, it seems, too stiff, corroded, to do the rock and roll. He's a sea story, like them all – the heart of darkness, drowned and eternal. The waves – like ghostly furrows, up and down they go and nothing grows ...' and Nestor interrupts,

'No, no, there's fish. They are the harvest,' but I go on,

'The fish swim in and out his eyes, he doesn't flinch, he doesn't blink – he turns the party on, snug in his bunk, the ship drives on to ruin, and he drops, quite vertical – and bloats, and up he floats ...' and I'm entranced, like Nestor, as I see the captain, white, a seahorse slowly trotting up the shore, his devil hooves a-burning in the sand.

'That may be so,' says Julie, unconvinced, 'but our Intelligence – it's paper money, bonds. You have to trust it – or there is a grand explosion; down the palaces! Smashed the Maseratis and the Cadillacs, all rubble for the dump! If it works, intelligence, there's peace, and trading futures, all that stuff—'

'I'm not intelligent,' I interrupt, 'I'm just a monkey, working there,' and Julie laughs,

'Of course, my treasure, little ape, I'm here to raise you, and carry you up the ladder of enlightenment. I buy you up – pure speculation, you must understand.'

I stare over at Nestor. He says, 'How we live badly here. There's no intelligence, no cash, and not much food.' It's so. This town – it should have stayed as fields or scrub. Or steppe.

I say, 'There's a lot of sadness here, cold sad, hot sad.'

'Well,' says Julie, 'there's not much we can do about it.'

'This hotel – they made it unsinkable. It's the last in town,' says Nestor.

I'm irritated, 'Julie, someone must be giving you those tapes – of the dancing, and everybody having fun.'

'Of course!' she says. 'Why, you're brilliant! You should go work in the field,' and she laughs.

'You don't have to force yourself, you know,' I say. 'Loving me, and that. Duty goes so far – that guy they play on the TV – he said they killed the children because they felt it was a duty then.'

'Yes, I know,' Julie says, suddenly solemn. 'I know. I feel sorry for all the others too. And the guy, the guard – he wasn't even a communist. Just a math teacher.'

Nestor reacts, as if we're criticising him – 'Now,' he says. 'Hold on. Math isn't to be confused with science. It's a different track entirely. The Indians worked that out before they got the motor car.'

Here comes my judge.

Julie defends me, and she says, 'This guy, my lover Jan, he has to have his trial. There can't be punishment. Here, we're not responsible for anything. Jan's head remains his property, sacred, inviolable.'

'Well,' says the judge. He stretches out, here is his home: my! what big boots he has, bought at the store ... He says, 'There's lots of sacred things around. The fish. That nomads do not eat. Respect. Respect so, too, for the spirits of the drowned. And those guys we see...' and he points across the icy furrowed lake, ice-fishers frozen on their holes, unmoving black and khaki turds – maybe a cage, a useless cormorant, beside – over to the isle, the faintly thrumming towers, and says, 'Our operatives, all leaping on the shore in glamorous fig. Julie, my dear, my longed-for love – you screwed up everything, the helicopters too. There's whole new companies of guys that's more than good, full of respect for everyone, that want to join our squads. Instead – the lake is frozen quite unnatural, caught in a magic blink. And shall they walk, these new recruits, across the floes?' And Julie's flustered, she must improvise:

'Dear judge! The battle's joined, the cash flows round and round. The bad guys wax and wane, it's like another moon – now they're our allies, now they blow us up; there is eclipse and falling stars and meteorites. There's hunter's moon, and there it looms blood-red above our bed, and blue moons too – they come and go, it's mystery: we quiz, we do not cure, our destiny.'

'And so?' asks the judge. Nestor here shakes his head, astronomy is in his bones, analogy and metaphor as well. 'No, no,' he whispers. 'Not like that at all,' but Julie says,

'The island guys – the tempest passed, the sound above them, a roar so terrible – a chord that's seldom used. Inspired, they were. The cure – it came to them – was Rock. The good, the bad – it's all a name for battling, struggle eternal, infinite. Religions, shamans – all insist, you love the good, and hate the bad. But bad is what you do. It's nicer than the good – and so the preaching's all a farce. You do the opposite to what they say you should. The good – that's me – is always moving on, like fish beneath the ice. You snag it – but it's dead. You throw it into raging oils – it's eaten, and it's gone! But being bad ...' She hesitates. The judge says,

'Yes, obviously, bad's fun, and profitable, moves the cogs around. That's why I'm here ... Although – there is no punishment.'

'Music,' she says, weakly it seems to me: 'And dressing up. It is another way.'

Nestor shouts, uninvited, 'There is punishment – but not from the judge! It comes to all, unearned and personal.'

'Yes, yes,' the judge says angrily, 'but we're not talking of that kind. It's Intelligence that we invoke. Things, contexts, settings. What people want, and can't get. Intelligence – that should guide the wanting, not this rock and roll.'

'No roll,' says Julie – 'just the Rock, the standing still.'

These court procedures, and the language! It makes you think of fishnet tights, and patchouli, and music all the night.

The judge says, 'This guy, Jan, doesn't seem to have done anything in particular.'

'If you can judge one thing, you can judge them all. That's what your job means,' I tell him.

He says, 'I go around the world. The thing is this. You must, each and everyone, be able to buy our stuff. And travel to our shops. And write down what you think of it. That's all. That's it.'

'So,' says Nestor, 'Intelligence doesn't come in at all,' and the judge says,

'No. Not to that bit.' We are silent, there is more mystery to be stripped bare.

'The harder part,' the judge goes on, 'is motives, and the consequences,' and I say, 'That's quite what I said,' and he says right back, 'That's where intelligence comes in. Not the finding out, what they might be. But judging. That is tough.'

'You must tell us all your moves,' says Nestor, dryly. 'The motives and the consequences. That chain.'

'Yes, well, he can do all that while we walk to the island.' Julie says. 'I'll get to see dear Erik. I wonder who brought their instruments?'

The moon is bright, white but tiny. Anyway, there's not much to see. The water should be flat solid – instead, it's held in furrows, rough and lumpy. The fishers light their lamps, they drink their vodka. Some have blood beside them, on the ice, fish in a basket, dead.

Nestor hums – '*Wir arme Leut*, we poor folk,' and I know it, but I forget where it's from. He doesn't tell me, and the music on the island grows ever louder, as we climb and drop, furrow after furrow – maybe soon the scene will flatten out, but on we go, down, up and down again.

Our desks packed together, make a stage. The music's in a pause. There's Erik, holding on to Julie – his arms enfold her, and he shouts – 'We're all stood down! It's over – lists, bad guys who travel round to raise some cash. It's armies now. The battle's on – time to enjoy!'

It's true. My uncertainties have flowered – the guys are clashing everywhere. Bands and militias. Almost everyone who's on the march is good. Not the time for delicacy, the individual case will certainly be heard when all is new and fresh, not now. It's hobby time. They're all on leave; before their battles, it is culture time.

Julie says, 'Yes, this is the moment. There's little wars all round – maybe they'll stop the big one so. Going to war? No, not for me, I don't want. Jan, you're compromised. Erik's a cop, so that's done for him. Maybe he's the one for me ...'

'Goddam, Julie,' I shout. 'The guy's a glitterbug! And besides, you made the running, you came after me, the disc, eating those goddam fish I'd made ...' I shout some more. Julie says, quite chill,

'Well, if it comes to that, Jan, you didn't make or even catch them. That was Nestor ...' Nestor says,

'No, Julie, I took them from a guy – the nomads, they respect the fish, so they don't kill them ....'

'Look,' says Julie. 'How the moon is bright, white but tiny. It must be minus forty here. The ice – it should be flat, instead it's furrowed, caught in a fold of instant, like a print, a freeze. Anyway, there isn't much to see. It is the pause, the music stops – it is the time you can decide, who to go on with. Take a side, a cause. Or maybe not, you all here being compromised, or not quite adequate for what you did.'

Erik charms her: a snake – both bobbing with his clarinet. Out it comes, viscous, the rope of notes, like lengths of liquorice, those bootlaces. Julie is trussed in them, black thongs, he drags her up the shore. She quite protests, but looks back, resigned, at me. Well, it's my moment too, the moment to decide. Here's Nestor tugging at me, 'Away, away,' he whispers. 'The thing is crumbling, as things do. The folk is fighting to be free, and then they'll bind themselves again. They wave their guns in victory – and then they slope them, off for some new territory, for orchards with the shade they'll never lie beneath, for ports where they'll row galleys. You can hear that beat right now ...' and it is true, the band – the big band now – is striking up. Julie's in a black cocoon. I must decide. He says, 'You see – the flags of triumph – soon they'll line the funeral routes, then down the warriors go, the earth – it's black and sticky, when you burst the shroud, it comes in on you, tastes of liquorice and fills your eyes.' And Erik shouts, that what they think is freedom is the order that must come. You break the tyranny, then set up your own. And it's rightly so. That must be, or else there's nothing, just waving flags and putting heads on poles ... That's what life is, eating the nasty stuff that makes you strong and well. The battle – it's for order, and for nothing else. And Julie says that's what she's always lacked – she knows what's suitable, but that is opportunism, maybe Erik's right, she needs the cops ...

'No, no,' I shout. 'There must be more,' and I don't think of what it is, but surely Julie's right to see her destiny in me, a journey we must make ... and there's the band, all glistering and dancing to the devil's tunes, it steams there in the cold, and there's the fishers, sitting like gophers on the silver lake.

I seize Julie, pull her from her bonds. Nestor shouts, 'It's a mistake. It is your great, your historical, mistake.' Julie shrieks, she's born again. She says,

'There is no choice – now we shall have to live by crimes. Away, away,' and Erik curses and he scowls, but, my! she's strong, she pulls us off the island, me, Nestor – and the band plays on and on. And up and down we trudge, over the furrows. We look back. The lake has flattened out. It's all as it should be.

'You see,' says Nestor, 'even the band is silent now,' and Julie says, no, no, it's just the distance, and he says that's exactly what he means. There's silence here, it must be minus forty, and the moon – smaller, and smaller, and our breath shapes up a cloud that hides the starry sky.

'Nestor,' I say, 'we lost the judge.'

Nestor says, 'He is contented, now, he plays that toktok, in the band. He helps the guys, he counts the beat. They play the numbers, and of course, there is no summing up. It starts, and

ENTERPRISING WOMEN

then it stops – the music. There's no judgement, and no commentary. It is better so.'

'There's no decision, then,' I say. 'The judge, the captain, they just play accompaniment, they drive it all along ...'

'And then they jump out – boo!' says Julie. 'That's how it goes – they can resolve, sort of, when someone's time is up. And – oh, how I'm missing Erik, that red hair ...'

'Is black, it seemed,' I say.

'They shave their heads, and paint the colour on the stubble – that is quite suitable, the fashion too,' she says, and Nestor whispers, that oh dear, she only judges what is suitable, and so can never fix her mind on this or that, on you or other, takes it how it comes ...

'Nestor,' I ask, 'do you suffer? It seems so. How much? And why?'

'Just think,' he says, 'if we lived in certain galaxies, our brains might all be joined up, a relay of them – how we'd suffer then!'

'But ecstasies – they'd be explosive,' Julie says, and Nestor shakes his head,

'Above a certain pitch – it hurts. It blows your fibres, and you come apart.'

I say, 'The band – spies, cops, assassins – it is doing well: it's called The Flames.'

'That's not the kind of truth we want to hear,' says Julie. 'Nestor goes deeper. Jan – I've quite gone off you. It's your fault, too.'

'Well,' I say, 'we have a way to travel. How'll we manage that?'

'With our good faith,' she says. We laugh. Nestor says,

'That's why the nomads sing, when they have packed their house, and take the track. They know that talk of truth and personality – it leads to battle, so – there's no truth in what they sing, except the song itself.'

We think about this. On our map, we see we're stuck within a mass of land, of soil, we cannot float and drift to somewhere else, and Nestor says, 'It's tragic. When you sail, you slide in everywhere, the maps say sea is azure, like the sky, the starry sky, and as you sail, you never hit a star, nor yet a piece of earth ...' and Julie says,

'That's not at all what I had heard of ships. They're always running into things – earth, air – it seems to be the same for them. They're blind, the captains, cowards all, and traitors too, I bet, down in their bunks, they dream of stars that draw them on like mermaids, to the rocks,' and Nestor says it is indeed like that, but now a truth irrelevant. We have no ship.

'I feel,' he promises, 'I suffer too,' and Julie strokes his head, and kisses him.

'No!' he says, 'not that. A gift that I don't want. It's true we sailors always look for somewhere to tie up – but we'll away – we always do. The leaving's part of the arriving, Julie,' and she says,

'There must be something more—'

He cuts her short. 'Guys who talk like that think they've got some answer, some fresh gift. They start from their conclusion. It's not a question, it's a prayer,' and on he goes: black matter and the galaxies where all our brains are set in relays.

'Enough,' I say. 'It's true we're disappointed with each other – but hear the sound of gunfire, down the street from Grand Hotel! The band that plays amidst the lake – The Flames

– they're now marooned, the fishermen are in the deep. It's all as it has always been – the battling. The new – it is The Flames, and they – ephemeral as ice.'

'I remember,' Nestor says, 'when it was the communists.'

'Well, we have problems more immediate,' says Julie, 'like where to go. Those firecrackers down the street – some celebration or a death, I guess. All seems to cancel out – the things Jan did, and Nestor didn't do. It's all too soon to tell, of course, they always say, and yet some things we're quite certain of, here, and on the island. Once it was the states too strong they feared, now it's the weak ones – I suppose there is no contradiction, ever, when it comes to judgment time ...' and Nestor says, 'No, no – it seems there is no contradiction here, but good and bad, they cancel out.'

'First it was the sociable, the socialists. Then, the godly. We wouldn't fit with either,' I say, trying to mediate: 'Or with all the rest. What battles they had, we had! Now, there's the interval. Rock. It's dead, but it will die again. Will Rock bring massacres, or just fade quiet?'

'Oh,' says Julie. 'Let's not go into the personality stuff. Character – I did all that with Erik. He was keen – lumping people together into groups, he said – it makes them round. Without that, you're just lumps. But I'd prefer to leave it all to luck – don't join a band, a group, and they won't load you on the train, or in the truck.'

'It doesn't work like that,' says Nestor gloomily. 'Some of my family had Nansen passports, didn't belong to anyone – they couldn't get in anywhere. They never docked, just went round and round.'

I'm something of a hero, I believe. Now, we're quite uncomfortable, it's true, just temporary. Out there, on the island

– I saved a heap of lives. The wrong ones, so they say... Maybe it cost a heap of lives – but then, things cancel out at worst. And now, this interlude, The Flames, waiting for something else. Everyone, two steps back – it's my doing.

Julie didn't tell. Maybe hers were the uncertainties. Nestor was the guy who should have been the punisher. Perhaps I should have gone overboard, but curiosity won him round. Well, what is his science, if it isn't walking in the dark, towards the darker black; behind, all's unseen, unseeable? Probably it's black. All complicit, all betrayers.

'Some of these houses have been burned,' says Julie, as we saunter on.

'They weren't much to begin with,' Nestor says. 'Others are just empty.'

'More of Jan's work,' Julie says, nudging mischievously.

'You stick your thumb into the works, it gets torn off,' says Nestor: 'Let's go down there – there's smoke rising: from eating, not settling scores.'

As we go, Julie asks me, 'Do you even know who it was you helped?'

I say, 'You have to help. You never know who. Not exactly.'

Nestor says, 'That's old talk. Guys that help now don't take sides. They're good indiscriminately.'

I disagree. 'Most still take sides. Often it's irrelevant – outside the little province.'

'You took the wrong side, Jan,' says Julie. 'That's what is interesting. Wrong for us, and wrong for you, because you weren't supposed to.'

'You need conviction,' Nestor says. 'That's a lot of being right. Then, if you back off, it gives it weight, it's not just scribble. I've conviction: we all took the wrong turn ...'

'Look!' Julie says, 'The Flames – are off the island. Their big concert.' There's the poster – the judge, holding up his blocks, the captain – his sticks. 'Erik!'

'Well, Jan,' Nestor says, 'if you were wrong, it's done. No regrets, I guess.'

'Whatever you did, Jan,' Julie says, 'it resolves nothing. You just confirm the stalemate. But me – I may have lost my job! Just for you; a feeling. Quite ephemeral, I'm sure.'

It's certainly not noble – none of it, and not her, not me. We're at the Grand Hotel. The guy says,

'Your bill, your wage – they're just the same. They cancel out. My! what a surprise!'

Julie pays our tickets for The Flames. 'Who's the glum ones?' Nestor asks.

'The ones that wave their arms is those that burnt the glum ones out,' she says. The faces of the audience, they all look the same, expressions sort them out. I guess it's dance and epic that has set them battling.

The Flames are hot. The captain and the judge, they drive them on. There's even bits of Salomé thrown in – 'No!' Julie says: 'I shall not dance – but I may have their heads. Just to keep,' and there is Erik, in the front, he bobs, emotes. And Julie is the snake who should rise naked from the basket, uncoil to two metres tall, and waver so.

Nestor says, 'This Rock is solid – it's not going anywhere, unless it's pushed. If I'd dropped Jan overboard like I was told,

I'd have the cash instead. I made the sacrifice – he seemed to listen to my cosmologies. But – we might steal their bus, and leave this place. The band plays on and on ...' It's an idea. Julie says,

'The people here – they love the animals that's beasts and also birds – the senmurv and the cockatrice, the gryphon and the sphinx – they're often seen round here. Dragons – that's what you need – they fly – the mountains and the deserts, if you have to trudge, it wears you down. The band – it sounds like everything, like every instrument, in there too is every song – that's what guys want – the earth and air, hammer and eagle ...' On she talks.

The captain and the judge – they're tiring now, the rest are racing still, the beat is slowing, and the two – they start to tilt, their blocks and sticks drop down, and Nestor says,

'Yes, yes. It's like the ship. The engine stopped, and we went broadside ...' and so it is, again.

Down, down, they go, the deep where no one practises or sings arpeggios. The others stop. Erik shouts, 'Captain – you've failed us! see, the icestorm's here. And Judge! We're sinking! Sort us out – redeem some categories, not saving women and their kids, that's out of date. A principle we can accept, and then sit happy in our cage a hundred years ...' But they don't respond.

'The Rock – it is the moon,' shouts Nestor. 'It doesn't move, it doesn't roll, and so it doesn't start or end – it's us who circle it. And now – it's down, it's set,' and Julie says, 'The band's burned out ...' The Flames – they are extinguished, but the guys who had their houses torched, now – they run to get the stuff to burn their neighbours out.

'There, you see!' says Julie. 'Not the spies, the terror, it's the music! – that's what set the people off. Maybe now they'll see they're better off without the beat – it could be in their culture too. No music – that is best.'

The judgment's hard, but logical. Nestor says,

'That's nominalism, Julie. Flames cannot be the cause and then effect. Me, I feel for everyone, I suffer with them all, the guys who do, the guys who tell them what.' He makes a soothing gesture – 'Maybe – more scepticism: that is best.'

Dammit – here's Erik, sidling up. Julie asks,

'No hassling, Erik – but why did you decide to be a band? Forever, all of you?'

He says, 'It is more fun. Much, much more fun. The dressing up, the long ago. The thrust, the throb. The rhythm section let us down, it's true, but they'll soon pick it up. When you play the clarinet – it doesn't cost you, no one's suffering. And it takes your mind.'

Julie will go along with that: Erik says, 'The spying – it's an ignoble thing. And as for all the rest – the battling on – everything cancels out.'

Nestor says, 'It all reaches somewhere – a level.'

'Well,' Julie says, 'my job is to see you guys do the job right. I don't go further ...' Erik says again, they'll get it right: 'The band – they are my brothers. Now we'll go to China – there, the art is quite industrial and welded, or it's *giclée* – that means a spurt of blood. It's rude, as well. Mostly it's for export – we'll be different, we're the imports.'

Erik – that hair, scarlet and black, but his seductive style, commitment. Assurance too: 'all cancels out'. 'Of course, there are the punks,' he adds: 'Lots and lots, all over. But they don't impinge too much.'

Nestor says, 'China? Everyone will end up there – but it's not empty, it is not the West ... With all its gold to be dug up,' and he talks of climbing masts – the apple trees – in orchards of Ukraine, and playing bandits in the forests, then the sea – 'The best of all, no climbing now, just waves and endless moving on,' and Erik says,

'The bus goes every way, of course,' and then he shows us on a tiny screen, what looks like ants in their necropolis. 'No, no,' he says. 'Not ants. It's Borodino. Yes, it's tiny, but the definition ...'

Now he's scarlet, now he's black, cannons and sepulchres. 'Poor guys,' he says. 'All fighting for the right. Some for the wrong, of course,' and Julie – sure, she loves him, but love's a daily paper, every day there's news, inexhaustible and peppy, and she looks magnificent, an empress left over from Byzantium, and so we all decide – go West, to Europe, we'll be imports there as well.

In the back, the springs are shot, the bus rears up and down to waves and wind, and Nestor hoists his nose, expansive. Closes his eyes, smells salt.

There's devastation all around. What isn't burned is left half built. I have Bruckner in my ears.

'It's like they had a war, without the ammunition,' Julie says.

'Some guys here, they're not so generous with their crews,' says Nestor, and I say, 'There's lots of movement – not like our solemn nomads' "go and in due time come back". Here, they just leave.'

The band – they sing, happy as crows.

Julie says, 'It's not so bad. The sea won't cover here.'

Erik says, 'There is no terror now. There's armies; and the rest – it's all done by computer.'

'The deed, the physical, is always best, has the effect,' says Nestor. Julie, suddenly, she cries,

'It's because we are all animists. We all belong to one another. The captain to his sunken ship – and Nestor is his crew. Erik – has met three ends – with me, his job, and probably his clarinet, but still he's boss and lover too. Nestor's without water ...' and he interrupts – 'Yes, but I'll expose false tracks, science takes us into ignorance and black ...' and he seems satisfied with this: Julie goes on, 'Jan has lost his awful work, but Erik's still his boss, and me? Who owns me now?'

It is a challenge, and I think how spying – it all ended when she put me on the ship, and ordered Nestor do what he then didn't, for scientific reasons surely, then there is the judge – I hear him at the front go "*one* two *three* four", click the blocks. He owns me, sure, he owns us all, but it's reciprocal, no doubt. Erik shouts up to the front, the driver – 'Don't stop, don't stop,' there's groups of guys, they stand around and look for history, perhaps.

'Don't stop!' we cry. We stop. Those guys are a true wall: they cry:

'Those Central Asians! That's where all the money's gone! To arms, to arms!' They storm inside. Julie says, 'We've Kyrgyz plates, that's why ...' and now the band is arguing, with passports out, and justifying. Too late, too bad. The instruments are tossed outside, they're carried like a Saturnalia, the saxes' beaks like weary phalluses, the blocks give their last tok, the basses worn like crowns: 'These guys can't even play,' says Erik, as his clarinet is made a pig's foot, opening a case. 'That's all my stuff!' shouts Julie, but the guys have taken bras and microphones and such – they're marching, and the captain cowers in his seat, the judge would jail them but there is no jail, no cops, and Nestor says, 'That is the way with storms – these guys are messengers.' He's satisfied – the eighty-five per cent of dark we ended with has come, has looted – then he says to us,

'Guys here – reactionaries! They've nothing left but cultural stuff, and protest songs and operas—' and he'd go on, but now the bus is set alight.

We stand around. The flames abound, the bus is mostly wood.

The Flames – on the bus side – 'The European Tour'. The flames arrive, and off the scrolly letters flake. How sad, how sad, we think, but Nestor says, 'It's culture, this. And change of use for clarinets – it's all as old as pyramids. If you write your destiny, it will come to meet you, that is sure.'

I think, poor Nestor, lost the orchards, forests too, the wind, the waves ... What has he acquired? Maybe a sea chest full of bones, left back in Kyrgystan. Here, nothing. His murderous serenity – for he never had, and so he's never lost, the music. Only a grandfather, maybe, singing to the kozba. Rounding people up, chasing them through forests ...

Julie says, 'You should have liked my CD – now, you're left with stodge. Bruckner! You need a voice to keep you company, not just trees and rock – see how it burns and splits, that bus. Our transport – sinks and burns, and when there is no more, we stop. No, it's not home – those bandsmen, they'll go off and where they go is home, or they will call it such. I'm looking for a pastoral ...' she doesn't say, and yet I think I am not part of it. She says, 'An alp; making the cheese. Eating it all, for it's ignoble, sitting at a market stall. And animals that never die, that you don't have to kill. The things quite suitable, and made of wood ...' No Erik there, nor me. An alp, and down below, the roofs, and people quarrelling and stacking logs.

She's free of family, a country, and it's right she should be free of Erik too. She'd be a true captain of that huge Chinese ship that sailed around the world six hundred years ago, and brought back every other wisdom, now buried there, within the Wall. Nestor her crew, Nestor, turning his hand to death, then pulling back. Her awful job – the fingering of each and all. It's good I should belong to her – no buy and sell, a bond. My own strong point – the treachery, and then the punishment: first ordered, expected, then – await some consequences. See how it finishes, who wins.

'Julie, put on my coat,' I say. 'This shore is cool. My nomad's boots won't fit you.' We laugh. The coat is Afghan, like they don't make any more, but fifty years ago, the guys all brought one back.

Erik says, 'The guys here look hungry, feisty too. I miss my clarinet – but they have nothing. Their bourgeoisie has let them down, betrayed, and ran.'

'Well,' I say, 'don't stare at me. It's not just leaders that betray. If guys trust other guys, they have to take the consequence,' and Nestor nods. 'Those labs,' he says, 'brain surgery.'

'These guys,' says Erik, 'they're not ready – to take apart an army.'

'They should make their own,' says Nestor. 'That's the way. And be more godly too, just like my grandad.'

I say, 'Burning the bus – that was quite feisty – but selling those instruments, that won't bring them much.' Each lays out their thoughts about the way we want to live. Julie says, 'I don't see much that's suitable around.' There is a smell of urine –

probably that's no one's fault, and Erik says, 'Nature should be your guide. I'm for disorder, though my training says it's unavailing,' and Nestor says, 'I am for order. My experience of sailing is – you go ahead and in the end, you hit a port,' and we agree that things will balance out. 'All I know,' says Erik, 'is I don't want people to be like me: and these guys here – they don't want to be like anyone at all.'

'These guys say they want to work,' I say, 'but really, they want pay. And us – we can live rich, we can live poor, we've no nation, and no inter-nation. Are we the future? Or are we useless?'

'This is not the moment,' Julie says. 'We're going to live poor, and with no pay. Those guys – what they didn't steal, they burnt.' Here, there's a kind of castle. Full of tiny rooms. We have no food. No vodka.

'Is this a place to start my farm?' asks Julie.

'Don't be silly, Julie,' I say.

She says I'm silly, made mistakes, a big one every month, but still we own each other, 'Not to buy and sell,' she says, 'but stronger. Inevitable.'

'Must we stay around that judge?' asks Nestor.

'Not a real judge,' Julie says. 'Piergiorgio. Can't always call him that. He's just another level.'

The other guys pack in with us: I say, 'When it goes well, the judge's toktok is inaudible.'

We're in a big refectory. There is no food. Julie scratches on the stone: a statue, guy in plate armour.

I say, 'No, Julie!'

'Why?'

'It isn't yours.'

She says, 'If I don't do this, who'll know that I was here? What do you expect – someone to write biographies?' She scratches Juli – a long J, and adds an 'an' to make it Juli-Jan, or Julian.

'Leave it,' I say.

She adds 'derik, Julianderik.'

'We're off to loot some stuff,' says Erik. 'The judge will come along.'

'You'll waste your time, you silly boys,' says Julie. 'Oh dear! Erik – you're not silly too?'

The captain's here. He says, 'Never give statues names. Julian, the Roman emperor. An apostate, perhaps. But have no fear – I am the only spectre here,' and he laughs, the old sea-horse, a silty neigh. Julie and I – we pull the forests over us, and sleep. There are no ghosts, no food. No Erik. In his sleep, the captain says, 'Nestor! Oh help me! My ships all sink, I'm rescued by barbarians – oh, let me sleep, hear, hear the deep ...' and maybe we do, and the longing too – that is for sure.

Here's Erik, and some guys – 'All we could find – some kilos of red caviar, the guys here, they don't understand; white asparagus from gardens – that we stole. They're coming! – now, aloft Sire Julian, we must defend this place, the barbarians are after us,' and Julie says, 'Of course they would be. They live here, that's their food.'

Raw asparagus – inedible.

We prop the statue up outside.

'Oh no,' we hear them shout, 'our heritage. The statue! Back off, you guys – that's precious stuff.'

We hear the cry to save their culture. We're the barbarians now. The crowds pull back, they see their art, their values, under threat. 'Forget the fucking vegetables,' they cry, 'and that red gunk. What can these foolish sidemen from Kyrgyzia care, what can they know of what is fine and true in life?' And on they go. It's peace, perhaps democracy. We set the statue back, its value quite intact.

'Well,' Erik says. 'Medals all round. Defence of the Dark Tower – and all quite legal, says the judge,' and Julie says the other guys defended too, and Erik asks, 'And did the captain speak?'

'Oh yes,' says Julie. 'Mermaids that snuggle by you in the night. And all the ships that sink – it's destiny, you curl up in your bunk, the sea – it takes you, like an octopus, a squid, it draws you in its beak ...'

'Just fishy tales,' says Erik. 'What draws him to the deep, that our Intelligence could never find?'

'It's not his mother, so it must be death,' says Julie. 'And – we should take that Julian along – he's better than an atom bomb.'

'But heavier', says Erik. 'Maybe we'll leave him here.'

'What's to become of all those poor guys?' Nestor asks. 'This used to be a rich place. The judge says next it'll be "poor socialism" – but he's deluded. I don't think much of him, his laws. There's always worse things coming when you're on the skids, and waiting for some new guys to come and steal your vegetables and cut your throat, live in your house ...'

'It's sweet you worry about them, Nestor,' Julie says.

'No, it's just the history,' he says. 'You make an epic of your fall – it makes your people's life a hell for centuries. That's what interests me. The best thing is not to start off looking, but discover at the end what you've not got. You're always starting over anyway. History's just sailing round and round, not finding stuff.'

'Sometimes it's fishing,' Julie says. 'Yum yum – I could savage an *omul'*, right now,' and it must be true. We're hungry still.

'They've took our instruments and guns,' Pergiorgio the judge complains. 'Our top hats too. You don't need be in Intelligence to understand our discontent. Now, what shall we do, and call ourselves?'

Erik says, 'Perhaps – the Weird Boys. Dress in paint or rags, and dance to someone else's base.'

'Too nordic, and too Protestant,' Piergiorgio the judge says. 'Besides, these guys here can't pay for concerts. They steal. And where's the cops?'

'If they're not here, they're somewhere else,' says Nestor wisely.

'Our guys have torched some houses. Like they do,' says Erik.

'Maybe Brazilian,' says the judge. 'My wooden blocks frustrate – I fancy something long, organic, that you stroke with steels.'

'That's all inaudible,' says Julie. 'If you don't drum, you're lost. Try stripping off and putting on some paint – they'll see you then.'

'It's the goddam captain,' says the judge. 'Batters those skins like he was flogging tars.'

'We need to find some guns,' says Erik. 'Put some new numbers in our heads – and then we'll need an agent.'

'Yes! That's what we need,' says Nestor. 'It always goes this way. You find a place that's in decline. A family becomes a clan, and then a tribe. You burn the place, then build your empire, all new palaces and such. Here, we have a judge, a captain, all these spies, assassins, diplomats. All we now need is someone to write it down, and lots of kids.'

'Well,' Julie says. 'Just count me out. Don't even think. I'm not a mother goddess, industrial breeding – not my thing.'

'The agent is important too,' Nestor insists. 'To get the gigs, be father to us all.'

'Not many pop groups founded dynasties,' says Julie. 'Or even built a house.'

I say, 'We're poor and unemployed. Not angry yet, enough.'

'The anger is the thing – but Jan, in any case, our guys will never let you back,' says Julie. 'Once you betray, the game is over. You're the apostate, like Julian there. Even if you flagellate, they won't forget. Erik, now – he'd be a chief, but I am stuck with you as well, the other side.'

'Julie,' I say later, 'something troubles me, while we're talking of the origin of the state ...'

'Oh no,' she says, 'the state is quite different, it comes much later, not always for good ...'

'Good for what? For who? Is this your joke, Julie?' I ask. 'What troubles me, since we are bound together, as is were, so well ...'

'Yes,' she says, 'the ownership.'

'Whatever it is. Did you tell Nestor to dump me overboard, back on the lake?' I ask.

She answers at once: 'Well, if you'd done bad, and the consequences were bad ... it's like what could happen to you, or all, or any of us – but it didn't happen. Nothing happened.'

'I got Nestor's cosmological perspectives,' I say. 'It doesn't seem quite satisfactory.'

'Well, it wouldn't,' she says. 'I wouldn't let it bother you. I don't.'

Erik overhears. It is his job. He says, 'Well, Jan, where's your good guys now? You screwed us up, and now, you'll never play your rattle in my band.'

'You know, we all do bad – you have to go with what guys want. That is the test,' I say.

'With what they say,' says Erik. 'And the rest is scrambled eggs.'

'I know you're sore you've been redeployed. Not all my fault. Besides, the guys are fighting now, so what's your scope?' I ask.

'Maybe a gold – even a platinum disc,' he says, and Julie hugs him. 'You bow before the wind – it blows from every side, and you must blow as well, and drum, and twang your strings,' and there I see his greatness, one who'll dance before the ark, or stuff it full of animals, or any goddam thing – I start to say, 'I love you, Julie, anyway,' but she is nibbling on a stalk, the white asparagus, and we are stuck, right where we were.

Alone at last

'Well, two people can't be alone,' says Julie. 'Jan, you're very quiet, but I see you there quite clearly.'

She's found her meadow, high up the mountain. I've nothing I can do. I ask, 'Our strange old jobs – harassing people ... the secret lake ...'

'Erik was a soldier, and a priest. Don't worry, he couldn't touch me!' says Julie. It's quite unlikely. Erik has conviction – going after the bad, not just bad guys. I've seen him, anyway, touching Julie, in quite a normal way – it's himself that is untouchable. Who'd want to nestle close to him? I say, 'We live off carrion. We're like moths around a murder. A murderer. Nestor – how did you see him?'

'Oh, salt of the earth. And sea. A fine worker,' she says.

'And they all went for pop,' I say. 'Where does that end?'

'Oh,' she says. 'The Flames, the Weird Boys, all that. Who knows where that's supposed to lead? Just playacting, I expect.'

'Nestor was wrong,' I say. 'Even if our science is all crap, it's a torch you carry as you march on in the dark.'

'Jan,' she says, 'you miss the point. Defending something, that thing, that core – becomes more concrete. What starts as chivvying, ends as being good and right.'

'That's what you say,' I say, to end the talk.

We found this hut, away from people, and The Flames; maybe we'll stay here for ever.

'Why don't you sketch?' asks Julie. 'Or poetry, if you can't draw – the noblest art.'

'What will you do? I'm hungry still,' I say.

'You remember, I said "the alpine meadow, the hut. The cheese"?'

'Your dream, yes, I remember,' I say. 'How long now for the cheese, and something with, perhaps?'

'Days, I think,' she says. 'There's animals to get.'

'When we're real low,' I say. 'People'll come from where they live, and give us work. Work – we haven't put it our poems and the rest – not for many many years.'

'You wouldn't want it anyway,' says Julie. 'They'd ask: "How many lines today? How much did you write? Or draw?" Look at the insects, doing what they know. Work? It doesn't always happen like you say.'

'Julie,' I say. 'You're just a child. Living on cheese. That's what the moon is made of. An afternoon of living off the land, we've barely managed that ...'

'It was the healthiest thing that I could think,' she says, briskly. 'Off we go! You better mend the hut door that we broke.'

Is this a type of pastoral? Down the hill. The townsmen spit – it seems at us, but maybe they have dusty mouths. 'We're leaving, thank you,' Julie tells them.

'Next, Julie? The guy who said, "a person's life is a succession of fortuitous situations" – he knew about it all,' I say: 'It's data – what you cancel, you've seen anyway. How does it end? The waves give you a destination, not just up and down. Which shore do you end up on?'

'No need to be angry, Jan,' she says. 'I'm paying for you, what I have. Everyone you've ever had a contact with – they discount you from the start, and everything that's going to happen too. It's all a contest. Over quickly. Like Turkish wrestling.'

There's not much choice – we'll meet up again with the group. Julie says, 'Be calm, Jan. A lake has just one shore. It's reassuring.'

'No, no,' I say. 'That's not at all the case.'

Coming Home

Here's Piergiorgio, the judge. He says: 'It's ending here. It's ended, really. Vanity, vanity. The soldiers will go off – they always find someone to fight, somewhere. But we'll play on. We dance. That's what we know to do the best. "The band passes by ..." You remember that? Brazilian.'

I ask, 'How's Nestor? And that Erik?'

'Both with new women,' Piergiorgio says. 'Nina and Flo. And us – we are the messengers. So many gangs like us, roaming the continent. Being the eye of God – that's all over – till the next call, that is. Only the traitors like you, Jan, you do some justice – hoping the skies will fall. They do, they have, but not for you.'

He's painted up. 'The body, that's where it all starts,' Piergiorgio says. 'We do man's whole story. Brotherhood as well.'

I say, 'Nakedness doesn't always mean the same,' and swift, he says, 'No, no. We've got pink tights.'

For sure, spying was a less noble task than this. He leaps, he bounds – so do the rest, it's Erik does the lights. He says, 'We've been stood down. All's in the open, the lists you screwed up, Jan – they're no use now. The dance! Who knows where that can lead?'

They're like pink fauns, all playing in the dusk or dawn. There's monsters off, a guy with swords – he pirouettes, maybe he swallows one, or is it just the light? The crowd – it sways and claps, and someone waves their arm. The bucket for the cash comes round, most scuttle off, but some guys give.

'Julie,' I say. 'I feel I'm in an envelope. I've this desire to innovate, to get away – to build, to found, to settle, to convert ... Somewhere like an Isfahan, but larger still: a new religion: a new vegetable. Things like that – and so you send the missionaries out, and then another batch to say it's all a scam. And you – I don't know you at all ...' and then she says,

'That's the best way, Jan. Is not to know. Put people you don't know upon a list, and see them run. Or squeal. Repent or fight. The rest, they say, is history – the knowing. And besides – the things you want – they've all been done. Persepolis, the tallest tower, the dance, the song, the prayer – back to the silent body, then you paint it up – those guys, Jan, that broke out of their box, it isn't just the new they want, it's other things, that's quite beyond you – start with cash; and then the fame, vainglory, one step more. Those things you can't aspire to. Or the poem you can't write, a secret tear that's bottled, hidden in the sand – they dig it up when you are sand yourself. That's what you leave, you idiot.'

'Do you rejoice, then, Julie?' I ask.

'You can't do anything of all your dream, hallucination, nor can Erik, do what he wants. The judge – he has no book, so he just says the little that he thinks – there is no rule. The captain's moribund again ... Insist, and you will all end bad,' she says.

'Rejoice, Julie?' I ask again. 'We're all fit to our purpose, it would seem, so you are justified?'

'Yes. Yes of course. It's better to be sure,' she says.

Here's Nestor's woman: he says,

'I found her in the forest. She is dark, you see: quite gothic.' And he hums, 'In the forests of Lithuania'. The judge says,

'She was picking poison berries for her husband's dinner.' Nestor laughs:

'It's novelty – she's not called a fire-eater now. She spits,' and he shows her front teeth, the gap where the stuff comes out.

'It's like that with them all,' I say, but without a pause, she throws her head far back, up and up there goes the flame.

'Nina, that's brilliant,' Julie says: we've black flakes around and on.

'I won't teach you how,' says Nina, quite graciously.

We see Flo, Erik's girl, far off. She's silent, sits like that Danish mermaid on the rock. There is no sea, no prophecy. Nestor says, 'Where does she stare? The future? Is that how you see? What a bore she seems,' and Julie says,

'Poor Erik! He would be a martyr for a cause. But – just another victim ... Dear me, how sad,' and she throws a stone to make Flo turn and look. Flo's back – that is her most fetching side, and golden hair, to lure you on, far from the shore.

'Come on, come on!' There's shouting – it's Piergiorgio. He says,

'We tried revival. Then, the universal message. But – the guys keep fighting. We should be convinced, our destiny is spying, judging – back on the island, choose a side, a history. Maybe it's our act, it hasn't caught ...' and indeed, the bucket's almost empty. We are hungry still. I say to Julie,

'Well, my dear, you fill a space. Maybe you are a space.' She's angry, and she says,

'I tried to make you useful. Punishments, rewards – you're always hungry. Has your life no interest for those outside?'

We find a haywain, that will hold us all. Flo sits on the tailboard. We just see her back. On to the silos! – that's the cry, and Nestor takes the reins, the captain sleeps upon the straw. The horses follow stars and meteors – we wander till we see the store, there's nomads' boots still outside, for sale.

But – where's the lake? The island? There's just a hole, with rusty hulks, the silos crumbled, like baguettes, there's sand,

and salt in drifts, like dandruff on a yellow shirt. The place is wiped out, closed, drained out, a sink. We're all aghast – not that we cared at all for lake, nor fish, the brothers to the *omul'*.

'You fishbone!' Julie shouts at me. 'I love my Erik, but I spend and waste my time with you,' and Erik says, now the facility is closed, it means there's universal conflict. He must go and find his destiny ... And Nestor says it's true, the biggest armies get most use; before you go, you may as well be armed and fight, impose yourself on everywhere, and grasp some guy, before you go, and wrestle down together, and you bite his tongue, or hers, and chew the cheeks until you find the wisdom teeth, and force your weapon through their window bars, the ribs, then into tripe and sponge dessert, and hold so tight as they ... they start to fly, you see the colour leave the eyes – of course, the tongue can't wag, you've got the wisdom from the mouth, and penetrate the heart and all those honeycombs, and see the light of summer nights – it fades, it dwindles. And you've won. 'The biggest army wins,' he says. 'But it can't pay its warriors.'

'Well,' says Piergiorgio. 'We know who's got the biggest army, and most cash, and better wired and insulated. I guess that's Erik's bunch. So, Jan, where's yours?' I murmur that I've friends to see – I wander to the store, and buy some vodka – there's no nomads now. The Grand Hotel is empty too, but guys will surely come to stay and film the void that was the lake, and maybe put more water in and drown the frigate, and the captain too, over and over – and there's Nina, my, those arcs of flame and soot she spits, they fill the sky, it's like a curtain opening and rising, turning black.

Erik says farewell to Flo, she turns, and there's her back again, she must be staring shore to shore. I never see her face –

she's maybe like a Helen, pouting, no self-confidence, her epic gaze feeds back to tiny brains. He says,

'It's all Intelligence, that's all you need. I could have stayed with Flo. Or Julie. Julie loves me, but she's fixed on what's appropriate. That's not Intelligence. We must infer. It's not like wearing armour, like that statue, Julian. You're unprotected flesh. You feign apostasy, that's true, but then you do your trick – putting the finger on some guy. You are the wasp, and he's the sweetly rotten fruit.'

'Erik,' I say, 'the wasp may do good things, but is not bright, does not infer. And fruit that's on the turn – makes marmalade and such. It's not intelligence you use, it's probabilities and rules,' and Julie shouts at me,

'You beast – you spoiled his fucking farewell speech,' and she goes on:

'The guys, the Weird Boys – now they're off to war. They're colonels all, or generals, the battle's fought on many sides, with many aims and exits. Borodino. And you – no, Jan, you won't go, not at all!' She sounds cast down. I say,

'I'm sure you're right, my dear. But – that is rather good, for us. Here, the water moves about – it may come back, as nomads do, the lake refilled, the captain uncurling like a leaf; he takes command ... Here we could bivouac, upon the shore. And wait.'

'No, absolutely not. I've turned my life for you – and now I've quite gone off ... and you're indifferent ... I think now – no one owns any thing, or any one.'

'Well,' I say, 'there's always Grand Hotel for me. I'll find a place, right high and fresh. They'll fight it out below ...'

'It will all change,' says Julie. 'And besides, they'll rocket the hotel.'

'I'll turn my hair around,' says Erik. 'Find me some uniform. Attack, defend, the job is all the same. Jan here – he inferred there were some good guys somewhere – that's a wonder! It turned out, that was as far as he could go.'

'Yes,' Julie says. 'That was the surprise. I'd thought he could go on some more.'

Erik says,

'So, Julie, good luck with the cheese.'

'The cheese. Of course,' I say. 'Good luck.' We squint into the future: I say,

'The nomads maybe won't come back. And we may have some victory, then back to Bruckner, like it was ...'

'Yes, yes,' cries Julie. 'Church organ, alps above, the village lies below, and there am I, a lace cap on my head, for sure.'

Nestor says, 'I'll keep the horses – tend them, like I used to, long ago. One day – refloat the ship, and travel round the world.' He points his sailor's eye across the void. 'Nina's my weapon,' he says, and then there's flame all round us. 'Sorry,' says Nina, gruffly.

He'll need to fight the nomads for those horses, if they come and find the water gone, the fish, revered, departed. They believe in reincarnation, not a resurrection.

Erik will win some medals, kill some loyal kids, no doubt. Or himself be killed. No doubt.

'They'll get a good fight from me,' says Nestor. 'And the judge – he needn't hang around. There's nothing he can do.'

'Well,' says Julie. 'What's to become of me? I know all about mortality – the trouble is, that now, there's nothing that's appropriate. Except the struggle – and I can't.'

'Come, Julie,' I say. 'Of course you must. See, the Weird Boys – each off to join their side. The judge, Piergiorgio – he'll not be wanted for a while, but in the end, there'll be a part for him. The captain too – he'll drown and drown again. The ship's his cart, his bed – he cuddles down, oblivious.'

But she's not satisfied, and not amused: 'I want what they want too,' she says, quite petulant.

'No, no,' I say. 'It shouldn't be for you.' She walks away.

I go up to my room – it's where the servants lived. There's no one else. The town is almost empty too. The fish – of course, they've gone! I use the vast Grand kitchens to prepare my food. I watch the sun, its rise and fall.

Julie – she surely can't have been my adventure. Later, she says,

'This food thing, with you – it's a bore. And conscience too – for you, it's all inside.'

'That's how it is,' I say, 'for those who're not already picked. 'Hey, son, shoot that tiger', says the dad, and so he does, like all the other boys. You make your choice inside – it is the only way.'

'You have to let it out, somehow,' she says, 'Or it's enclosed. In stone, like Julian. You wear the armour – but you're stone. So what?'

'Julian is your invention, Julie. Lots of Roman emperors came here, and some would wish they'd stayed back home. But Julian – the lump we found – is nothing. No apostate, no apostasy.'

'That's just what I have said,' she says. 'You have to let it out. Besides, it's not only tigers that got shot. There's people running everywhere, just to avoid the bullet. Or the cage. Someone must empathise.' I say,

97

'Erik? Is that your thought? He's like those wooden soldiers, as a kid you lick and lick, some paint remains, and smells. Addictive. But – you grow out of them. When you grow up, there must be something more.'

'Still on about Erik, then?' she says. 'He did it all, the battling, first at a distance, now up close. Even the best, the very best, guys think torture is appropriate. It's not the worst, and anyway, in everything, there is a bit of it. Torture. I've found it so. With you.'

'Will you hang around here for a while?' I ask.

'I'm still one of the good,' she says. 'There should be the helicopter. They bought swarms of those. Who knows who'll come for you. Promising who knows what.'

'I could have promised them fried fish,' I say. 'But there aren't.'

'We're all good folks,' she says. 'We from the North. Not in it for the cash. Ready to give love – if it's appreciated.' I say,

'The captain's broke. No cash – but look at all the fights his ships were in.'

She doesn't consider this. She says, 'So long as Nina shoots it out, the fire, you're safe. So, I don't mind leaving you. Not a bit.'

I say, 'I like it here. It's quiet. There's not much to attract the guys, the dangerous ones – unless there was some purpose, reason, secret, not just absent minds, that let the lake go dry ... Go now, Julie, while it's safe. Do you remember – the bus they burnt, and being spat at? And the summer afternoon? No harm done to anyone.'

'Yes,' she says. 'I should go now.'

Krystal

I have a new identity. New friends. I'm supposed to care for refugees.

Alan's writing a Mass without belief. He says, 'If it seems odd, you know nothing of music, or the music business. You write something to create belief – expression alone is sterile. Now, I need something to make the cold. Cold of the spirit, when there is nothing new, no courage to start something over.'

'Tubular bells,' I say. 'Maybe you're right,' Alan says. 'Russian. With those high sharp voices.' We are to hear no more of tubular bells.

'It seems to me,' I say, 'there's not much new anyway in what you're doing.'

'Desperation. The search,' he says. 'You don't need safe haven to have those. Limitless.'

'It's ritual,' I say. 'It's the terrible thought that comes as you perform it: "I believe in the void." Although they say there's landfall somewhere. You could keep the titles of the pieces – use different words.'

Alan says, 'I prefer to keep the words and do dirty titles.'

We talk of Phil, our friend. I say, 'He writes fiction, I believe. How strange, and what a comedown. He was the best of us.'

Alan says, 'Everyone is into art. They're unemployed. They say about novels – there are unforgettable pages in some.'

I say, 'I've not come across those – but if you don't read the stuff, how are these pages unforgettable? It seems quite woolly. Some meals seem unforgettable at the time, but they can't be repeated, and four people may eat the same stuff, and three forget entirely. Or feel ill.'

'That's crap argument. You're supposed to breathe life into the characters,' he says. 'And dammit – there's those guys, your refugees, from Misery City, come to see us. They get the avant-garde stuff off the computer. They'll think I'm fossilised. It's the embarrassment too – the religious stuff they believe, and the fact we're occupying them.'

I say, 'Maybe they won't stay. They've no code for pretending they like foreigners.'

Salm and Ziad at home.

'This is the only house where there's no arms,' says Ziad. 'It'll seem suspicious if we're searched.'

'If they find some, you'll be taken seriously,' Salm says. Better live with suspicion. If they take you in – tell them lies. That you're a violinist. That way they go for your hand and leave the rest alone.'

Ziad says, 'You're sure? If there was that much certainty around, we shouldn't need to pray so often every day.'

Salm says, 'They've so many types of trucks, those foreigners – if you were a young collector, you'd go crazy for them. In miniature, of course. I see those people as landed from another star – you'd expect them not to speak your language, and to trash your house. It's not so strange. Just keep repeating that.'

'Of course this is a country, but being so hasn't brought us fortune. Maybe the next step ...' Ziad says. 'No, they're fixed on countries, the foreigners and our guys.'

'You listen to their religious stuff, Salm. Are they believers?' Salm says. 'Small things must be believed in by everyone. It's common sense. Big things – it's open season.'

'That's a wrong way round, somehow. Anyway, look how you dress – no one modern wears that stuff,' says Ziad. 'It's cool. And will seem cooler still in time,' says Salm.

Glass doors, or wooden ones? Glass, you see who's there, and hear the break. But wood keeps down the blast. The strike: Salm says: 'It brings it back, the stuff I've read. Workers and strikes. But the history – so slow, like marquetry. It's stirring – I mean, it stirs me. But the people here are not yet real. Whatever it's about, it's not about work and politics.'

'Well, you can't stop things once they're started, whether it's strikes or what they're against,' says Ziad.

'When we're away from here, we mustn't mention fear, or anger,' Salm says. 'Stick to art. No family stuff. People are tired of us guys being killed and blown up, and we've nothing new to say. Don't mention you're scared, they'll think you're some kind of moderate or renegade. And anger's out – they'll think we want to kill them.'

*

Salm and Ziad arrive. The four of us discuss the strangers' art.

'These painted blocks, Salm,' says Alan, my friend. 'And what looks like games – those strips you find on your computer. What does it say? What do you do it for?'

'It's been hard to leave the house back there,' says Salm.

'The strike – that's quite promising,' his friend, his brother, Ziad, says. 'Work and not having it – it makes a bridge.'

'Well,' says Alan, 'I'm sure you guys are at the leading edge – but I can't show you round. In the car – we four: we'd look like gays. I mean, gays quite of the wrong kind. Or sporty types. Imagine!'

There is more silence. Salm and Ziad more often look at each other than at us – they're not gays of any kind, it seems. Alan says, 'Salm – you look brighter than your friend there, Ziad. I bet you've riches where you're from?'

Alan seeks to find a neutral ground. The flattering of wealth.

'Why yes!' says Salm. 'A big compound. Gardens – we think they remind us of paradise, you know. With cranes and egrets, stands of bleached grass. Pampas – that's the word.'

I say, 'Don't mind Alan – it's just the way we kid around. Especially with other people.' I think of the girl in the bar this morning – she'd drawn her eyebrows to meet, like Sheherazade. I tell her so, but she doesn't recognise the name. She's Lebanese, French, Arab ...

Later, Salm says to Ziad, 'I can't make them out, if they're joking, or they're just crap. They'll never let us see their contacts.'

'They must have contacts, or they'd not be what they are. What they say they are,' says Ziad.

'It's back to cranes and egrets, Ziad,' Salm says. 'Those ponds are full of sharks, but in paradise – it's useless to criticise.'

'Ziad's gone back,' Salm tells me. 'The trouble is, you have to live in a place. All the rest – security, loving others, seeking recognition, goals – you can work out for yourself, alone. But breathing – you must do it in a context. Me, I'll stay here, and be illegal.'

'It's what I'd do,' I say. 'Usually you know about the laws you break, but being illegal, just being here and doing nothing, is quite new.'

'Someone will be found,' says Salm. 'That is the way. Food, a roof – most people have enough for two. My role to judge the portions, according to our need.'

A few days later – 'I've found the right woman!' Salm says.

'Not Sheherazade, I hope,' I say. 'I've still some future there.'

He goes on, 'I'm not humiliated so, taking some help. On the contrary, relieved. We must all get used to live in ruins. The guys from the next street, they're bringing ruins, more and more. The rhetoric comes under the door like sand, fills the house full. None of it exalts.'

Later, he says, 'You guys don't know how insecure you are.'

'Yes, I do,' I say.

'You think what's happening to us is just the past, lingering on. It's the future of us all. Best you start living in it, like us, like a ruined training camp. All our best stuff, plates and tiles, it's useless, trucked off, it's trashed, or somewhere behind glass. My uncle traded glass. That's the best material, the best business. Crystal should be better still. Much prized, it was, in China, jigging along on camel trains, long ago. The good life, the singing. Now, the big palaces are made of it. It keeps the cool air in. And when it's smashed – there should be uncle with his notepad, his estimates ... The good stuff – used to be inside. Now it's in some showroom, glass behind glass. Probably armoured, too.'

I tell him. 'People here – they want to send you off. Then, when you're home, they do surveillance on you, and say: '"Don't come back. Behave well."'

'We're quite innocent,' says Salm. 'You guys have had experience – the wars, civil and not, occupying, occupation. We're still with backstreet gangs and shifting sands.'

We pause. He says, 'If I'm sent back, you mustn't think I'm feeling guilty. Here's not paradise you're expelling me from. It's just my convenience. That's becoming inconvenient. We, we all around, we're your barbarians. Do you sit on riches we are greedy for? Do I plan vendetta? I doubt it. We might just leave you be, when you have done with us.'

I say, 'It's "we" now?'

'A convention. Nothing real,' he says.

Alan says, 'Who knows where they'd send me, if I didn't have a choir and my passport. That's what Salm needs – a show or two. They'll never get rid of him, if he flaps his wings.'

I say, 'I'm not concerned, I'm not involved. It's just people, avoiding heavy traffic, running. Of course, it's nice to see some reach the other side.'

He says, 'It's all a bluster and a parade. Stock figures. Crazy people, crazy stories. "*J'ai seul la clef* ..." to the parade. But we've all got the key. There's no door for the key – parades don't go on behind a door. We know all the stories, told every night. Don't save anyone's head.'

Salm distrusts Alan. He's right.

Alan says to him,

'You're afraid for your body, over there. Not your brain. And coming here – it's your body that's not liked. Not the space it might fill – there's lots of space. Not your brain, not your customs. Just you, you and your envelope, the lonely cadaver you inhabit. It's not liked here. So, that's why, if they knew, they wouldn't let you in. Try to send your brain instead, or your customs. That's quite ok.'

'No,' says Salm, 'It's my father. You can't locate him. That's what you guys want to see in us. Succession, descent. One after another, each holding a tail.'

Alan says, 'Don't try to mention persecution – that's your destiny. Ziad's doing all that part for you. No, you have to sacrifice your body. Bloodily, then make it disappear. Then we'll love you, revere you.'

I say, 'Salm's found someone to keep the rain off him.'

'I hope he's up to it, to all the tricks, as an illegal. I should denounce him,' Alan says.

'Alan,' I say, 'Remember, apocalypse is your thing. Not ritual, duty, all ready and cadenced. Think of your 'Kaddish for unbroken voices'. Think 'end of the world'. That's your big idea.'

He says, 'Music doesn't need big ideas. A small idea, worked into something structural, and a big ambition. That's the recipe. Gossip, too. And so... Salm's girl: she's called Krystal.

She likes his vision, and the romance of flight. That lets you fit in everywhere. She's a friend of Shusha – your Sheherazade. With her, you should go beyond the eyebrows. Anyway, she's too grownup for you. No money, but used to having it around. Probably, I should denounce you all – but that would make me seem puffed-up.'

Krystal wears a rainbow poncho. 'Don't you know how old that makes you look?' asks Alan. 'Needs a historian of the knitted shroud to give a date to you.'

Krystal laughs. 'It's ambition that I look for. And apprehension. Salm has both – a fierce desire to save his skin. His neck. You see it in his art – all holding back. Ah – if it were let out! Would break all circuits.'

Salm says, 'In my business, you read a lot about the ninja. I'd be like them. Muscular control, and maybe not existing. Walking along the corridors like pencil drawings on the walls. Anthracite the colour. Navigating the corners. Probably never fighting. Not having to.'

Krystal seems to be his agent. She explains, 'Yes, the *bande dessinée*, the strip. That's where Salm lives.'

Shusha says, 'The one-dimensional warrior.' It seems it's her joke. Hers and Krystal's.

Krystal says, 'Salm needs setting up: the right music, fresh kinds of clothes. Maybe a dog.'

Shusha says to me, 'You say you've special qualities. Move them into the light. See if they're like mine.'

I say, 'It's their rarity that matters. Not being plausible.' There's awkward silence, then I say, 'Perhaps I should ask about your family, Shusha. Though the history is always terrible.'

'There!' Shusha says. 'You know it all. Don't ask.'

'My character, "Salm",' says Salm. 'It's not me. It's a sketch on the wall, that moves round the corner, through the graffiti. The wall, the window – they fall, I'm still there, immortal, clinging on. It annoys the rest, the fleshy bodies – they're furious. "Salm" is immortal, mischievous, terrified. A sketch – it can't belong to anyone, can't have a family, belief or practice. That's lucky, and it's bad. "Salm" has no hand to give or shake, or promise peace, or pour a drink. No hand you can harm, either. You try to rub him out – he's quicker, and in the end – who cares? A drawing, skittering away.'

'It's nice,' says Krystal, who clearly doesn't think so. Alan has turned away. She goes on, 'But it has no strength. That "Salm" – it has to surprise, to snatch your wallet. Make decisions. Pay its way and make you think – that's a trick, but it's on the human side.'

'Those are all things I don't want,' says Salm. 'Exactly.'

I say, 'Krystal will make you great. Or full of cash, at least.' I'm holding on to Shusha when I'm saying this, maybe greatness and wealth appeal to her?

'Ziad is my body,' Salm says. 'He's my sacrifice, he does the suffering. I'm his sprite,' and Alan says, 'None of us has faith, that is OK. But you've no belief. We all have that. Good or bad. If you don't have it, you're cut out of everything, you're like those sandy stumps of stone, half buried in the sand. No reconstruction.'

'Just ruins,' Salm says. 'Lots of them. Building others every day.'

Later, I say to Salm, 'You've done well with Krystal,' though I think of me and Shusha.

He says, 'I don't see the point of old people. She'll be old, some time that may seem soon.'

'It is like that,' I say. 'Life, clinging to it. No one expects you to be a hero.'

He says, 'I've been reading epics. How strange, they named Paris, France, after that creepy Greek kid. Frenchmen! Really odd – they don't seem the altruistic type. Spilled their anger into decapitations. And Ulysses – those Irish bars! Not much to fight for there.'

'That's a different Ulysses,' I say. 'Though you could be right all round. As for foreign troops – they come in when you have countries ...'

'No,' he says. 'You're wrong, you think only of yourselves. Troops come in with families. You seem them strut and gawp at stuff, your stuff. So, you suspend your anger with the neighbours, those crap guys from next door. You must fight those real foreigners. We all agree – they're carrion. They never leave, they settle. Families.'

They've taken Ziad in, someone has. He's disappeared.

Salm says, 'You think: to disappear – that might be nice, and out of harm.'

'That's terrible,' I say.

He says, 'Krystal's supposed to compensate for that. She should be the goal, and the support: that's what the epics say. Or – just a story, gathering speed. Don't place a bet on Shusha – you may find the plot is full of sacrifices.'

Shusha is really smart: some of her stuff is leather, and smells new.

Mostly I, you, attach to short women, and if you're gay, to short men. You're always having to arrange the vertical to get along with them. Or, changing places, the short must find a way to climb the towers. With Shusha, here's her face, right there before you, your words go straight to target and come back, like from a slingshot. She says, 'Krystal likes being close to people working on some project. It could be a bridge, a jingle, a piece puffing something. She likes driving a load. She's good at that.'

I've nothing to say. With Krystal, it's not about vainglory or aesthetics, just driving somewhere. Shusha says,

'It's terrible about Ziad. But also good.'

I say, 'You're not supposed to creep around to bright sides.'

'Disappearing. It's a relief,' she says. 'That's what death is for. Relief, for the dead, of course, not for us.'

I say, 'That's what they all say to the dead. In Ziad's case, I doubt it's a comfort.'

She says, 'I like that about you – you don't say you'll help your friends. And your best friend is that shit Alan. I've always known shits. They light up EXIT – and out you go. The woolly ones, like Salm – they don't have anything at all that lights up. It's just some little scrawl that moves around the wall, bringing them respect, they think.'

'You can understand why he's evasive about himself,' I say.

'No one wants to be caught,' she says, firmly. 'But it's not world's end for everyone, if you are.'

I say, 'Alan can take a joke. An insult, that is, about his compositions. He knows how the business works.'

Shusha says, 'I have my plan too. I want to be a young very wise woman. No singing, no dancing. No store hours.'

'A white witch,' I say. 'Adulation from a stupid audience. Waiting for you to get fat or o.d. Then crying about it, all morning.'

'Well,' she says, quite excited, 'that's the aesthetic part. But that way, you don't disappear. The less you accomplish, the more likely it is you disappear and you leave no trace. Look into the history, most disappear. Make a noise – they'll carve your name.'

'Or do it in pencil, at least,' Krystal says. 'I guess it's me and Shusha – we'll have to go and search for Ziad.'

'Well,' says Salm, when he hears, 'of course I can't. Can't go look for him.'

'No, no,' Alan says, 'you draw your little character! What is he – the dead labour that enables living labour to get its daily crust? The past's inevitable, that's for sure. It's like religion, keeps you in its bonds, steers you straight on down the track. Until it can't.'

'Don't you fear?' asks Salm. 'The moment when it can't? My little creature, like a gecko, stuck on the walls – until it drops. The moment comes – the past won't work, can't drive, can't reproduce. Can't make the future. The money, spirit, that it represents – it stalls. The people tire of bowing to their god, and see that they can do without. But all around – there's just the sand.'

'Well,' Alan says. 'I'm sure your little scribble gets that straight. I've a commission ...' and again, this is his explanation, and his crest engorged with hope and pride.

'We didn't find Ziad,' Shusha says. 'That place – it's a depository. Boxes with broken guys inside, just waiting, praying.

110

What have they all done? And guys outside – what can they all do, have done?'

'You didn't go,' says Salm. 'I tell it from your eyes. Once someone disappears, going to look for them, you don't come back the same. That explains your fear – and mine. Besides, you wouldn't know how to look for something that's not there.'

'We both looked for Ziad,' Shusha says.

'In the air,' says Salm. 'I know you. That's where all the solid stuff has ended up. On your desks. Computer search. Your fingertips.'

'It's true,' says Shusha. 'We did a search.'

'Where you looked,' says Salm, 'it's graphics. A thousand stories. Nothing. No life, just a tale. Surviving the night. No Ziad.'

Shusha says, 'The word goes on, because there's contradiction, to infinity. There's always faithful and the traitors, yes and no. If we find Ziad in a story, well, that's something, he's been found! His story lives, immortal.'

'The word persists, Ziad does not,' says Salm, and Krystal says,

'Well, look at cash. It seems quite hard and round. And yet, it flies away, into the air, it seems, and gives us work. The future too. And if it stops – the future stops as well. Then, there was work, and now there's not. Once there was Ziad – now there's not.'

'That's crap,' says Salm, 'Ziad's not work, nor word.' We are silent. It's hard denying that.

'Ziad didn't mean a thing,' says Alan. 'Just another warrior. A dead one, too. Not fighting. Killed in the changing room, before he got his armour on.'

'Just – he didn't fit, superfluous,' Krystal says.

111

'The story's awfully sad. They always are. Uplifting too. But after all – things aren't about us being fair and just, it's me and Krystal getting rich,' says Shusha. 'Well off, they say.'

There's a crisis ...

'The goddam church,' says Alan. 'They say there isn't cash to pay me. I bet they still pray for getting paid themselves.'

'It's true,' says Krystal. 'I've hardly any money left. Salm should draw faster,' though she laughs, and Shusha says,

'My stuff cost lots. But no one wants to buy it off me now – that's good. I'll wear it to the end,' and she laughs too.

'I'm supposed to let it out,' says Salm. 'The anger and the loss, and shoot someone. But – it doesn't work that way.'

'It would be grotesque,' says Krystal. 'Though you're not exploding – it's a weakness in your art.'

'We'll tough it out,' says Shusha. 'Some continent'll get poor and screwed like us, then we'll take off, be rich and start it all again.'

'Yes, Shusha,' Krystal says. 'We're like a band. Our name persists. The dead ones, they just don't come on stage, the others make the albums, do the gigs. Invent, invent! The word, the words, the lyrics! Hey, you guys – think of something new and fresh, re-invent the old, and stir it all together!'

'Kissing in the rain' ... the song says.

The Solution

'My idea is this,' says Krystal. 'When the world is against you, you must make another. There's nowhere else to go, no other image. Shusha knows – more stories and your head is safe.'

Shusha says to me, 'You won't come into stories.'

'Well,' I say, 'I'm sure there is a bar for me to help behind.'

'Quiet!' says Krystal. 'Of course there'll be a bar. Vodka's what we need – and juice: red for Red Square, pineapple for the Abkhaz Sunset. The point is this: the show is called The Roof. We'll put it in a tent – that way, we save on rent,'

'And we'll rhyme too,' says Alan.

So, off we go. We're already all sorts of bits of history. Some of it – on the wrong side. Wanted the wrong side to win. We go far, far away.

'The Roof,' Krystal goes on, 'because it's to give you lift and panorama, like standing on the roof of everything. And then – the roof is over you as well, protects. So under it and on it – there is everything. There's art and bands and pictures, wise tales, opinions. Maybe Shusha's clothes – on sale, and precious things, quite overpriced and few. We don't want to work too much. Shopkeeping – it's ignoble, but we can turn a buck. And Salm, of course, will have his corner. All kinds of stuff to spy on too – friends and states, and guys in secret uniforms who come to drink and use intelligence on us ...'

'The *chic du chic*,' says Alan. 'Ugh.'

'Yes, yes!' says Krystal, quite enchanted. 'That's exactly it. A place you pay not to go in, and when you're there, you pay not to go out.'

113

'And do we think there are still men and women?' Shusha asks, 'or is it just for any curious people on two legs? Or none?'

'No prejudice regarding legs. Or any other thing,' Krystal says. 'All that is solid's questioned here. We pour the concrete every night, and in the morning – blow it all away. Pouf – like that.'

We pitch the tent. Opinions come from Shusha: every night a sultan with the power of death's appointed, and she saves her neck – she's thoughts on this and that and everything, and Alan hires the groups, wow, they are wild, he finds them in the alleys and the dumps – they shriek and girn, and way up high we hoist a cage – there's some wise guy on hunger strike, a conjurer, contortionist – it's hard to see – the guys are smoking finest grass, cigars in trunks from Cuba – there's a cult here of the body, prizes for the best. And Krystal cries – 'now, no excess, we make no profits, just hold to the beat', and beats there are, all kinds, a shrine to Ziad and all soldiers who're unknown, or missing, deserted, shot by their own side. We recreate decades that everyone forgot, invent some new ones, past and future; in the present, we don't linger, every night it slips away.

'More vodka and less juice,' cries Krystal, and I spike up the Squares and Sunsets, colour them with horses' blood and piss, the guys are avid, 'more and more' they shout – and so I pour it down them, till they swagger out, and take a turn, then back they're in for more.

'It doesn't change a thing,' says Alan. Shusha says that is the point, we've done with changing things, we pour the concrete in, and it may make a building or a bastion, statues and kerbstones, but in the morning – 'pouf', away it goes, you take a picture on your telephone – oh no, it's gone quite blank and silent, sightless, so you have to swagger in and out again …

114

'These guys have lots of cash,' says Salm, 'but not much judgment.'

We have no security, but then we see that guys drop in, Intelligence, and guys from armoured cars. They say they're there to keep us safe. Alan says they're interested in a tank he dreamed of – not the flat and portly ones that run around main streets, but little flexibles, like centipedes that sneak up alleys, back lanes, block guys good and bad that's running off. And Krystal shouts,

'Ideas, ideas – more rhetoric, swirl it all around,' and so we do, and there is contests for the highest kick, and corners for philosophers, and Salm is drawing, crouched and concentrated like a lady mantis, little males and gals in one-dimension sliding to and fro – the planet's tallest tower, the biggest shopping paradise, and Krystal shouts at him, 'No irony, no sarcastic stuff – remember Ziad and the strike, the wind that blows the tent and lifts it like a paper sack, and drops us ...'

'No!' says Alan, 'forget the ephemeral. That had its shaky day. It's us, solid here, and doing what we're good at. Not what we want.'

What had I wanted? I forget. This is quite good. A white space, to make a little money. To honour Ziad. Or the strike – something we couldn't do, and maybe didn't want.

We don't sleep: we work. Krystal says, 'That's tough – but the world, it slides around, it doesn't stop, it doesn't sleep, you never catch it out.' We don't feel well, but it is true – no one can catch us out. Shusha says,

'Salm should draw more – for people love to see the tale of good and bad, and judgements made, that prize the good.'

'Shusha,' I say, 'Of course I love you, and that's good. But Salm's little creature – it runs, that's all.'

'Hmmm,' she says, 'this love – I'm not convinced it falls within the good.'

There's always moonlight here. We take our breaks, as guys pile in the tent and out. 'No prostitutes,' says Krystal. 'In a tent there's no back room, and no upstairs. Desire – behind those bushes, please.' She runs a tight tent.

'Poverty suits Alan, softens his corners,' Shusha tells her, but to me, when Krystal's left, she says, 'Work doesn't suit you, though.' I tell her, 'I was not made for work, nor work for me.' The moonlight makes us look serene and wise, our faces ivory, our hair is grey like monkeys'.

'This pace!' Shusha says, 'I've almost no opinions left – each evening guys come in and argue and elucidate, for me, it's like a tennis marathon, I'm tested, and I run, I run upon my cube...'

'Be Socratic,' I say. 'Defend a concealed position. Start with dust, and end with dust.'

Shusha ignores this: 'Krystal's a great leader, don't you think. Quite inspirational.'

I say, 'She drives us like donkeys. We shall dry up like princesses in the desert.'

Shusha ignores this too. She says to me, 'You're not at ease with elegance.'

I say, 'Those watches we're supposed to sell? Absurd.'

'No, no,' she says, 'my elegance. Like the song says, "looking for the golden light". We looked for Ziad – there's so many people really there, and really lost. He wasn't there. How can you be lost, and not be found as one who's catalogued among the lost?'

'There's whole religions rest on that,' I say. 'Alan's the expert in what's not there two times. And always the answer's – "disappeared".'

'A dog,' she says, 'to humanise the place. My family – they had them, tall ones. It set us quite apart – from some. Then, they were everywhere. Elegant, too. It is the modern way.'

'It's true,' I say. 'We could be in China here. The moon is just the same.'

It's a romantic instant. Then, Shusha says,

'No, you're quite wrong. Look at the pictures, in China the moon is not the same. Just everything else – and maybe they have longer breaks.'

'No, Shusha,' I say, and laugh. 'It's certain we're in China. Over there, the village where they can't afford our prices. Some of those houses – fallen down, so soon.'

'There's lots of Chinese in tonight,' she says, offhand.

'And guys too, from Intelligence, like I was in,' I say. 'You know, there's sailors, airmen – but about them there's no trace of sea or air. It's just computers, every day. Like us.'

She twists away from me: 'It's time for you to pour again,' she says. 'Alan has these military dreams – it sets a tone discordant. Gets the wrong crowd in.'

Krystal calls: 'Hey, you two. Out of the bushes! I'll let you sleep lots, soon. But then – how'd I manage?'

Alan and Salm are talking about bombs – Alan has dreamed of them again, and planting them, and Salm is drawing smoke – they've pulled a crowd. There's Chinese tourists, some guys around from the security crew. Shusha says to me, 'There's not a family that I know that hasn't heard of bombs, been occupied. Don't ask!'

'Terror and being poor,' I say. 'They seem the same, but really they're quite different.'

'It's just the lack of sleep,' says Shusha. 'Maybe we should say to Krystal that we'll go on strike.'

I say, 'She'll just bring other people in. We are her friends. She is quite reasonable. She likes to manage people, usually celebrities, artists and such, and has them on TV.'

On TV, attractive people have some sex together, and it's on and over in a minute. Switch the TV off – getting sex takes days, months, even for ever.

'I hate those guys in uniform,' says Krystal, 'though I can usually tell who everybody is.'

She says she trusts me. 'I need someone with the power about them,' she says to me. I feel her poncho close, almost it enfolds us both.

'Well,' I say, 'it's true that Alan's rather idle. That band – it's been the same for months.'

'Oh,' says Krystal, 'I'd not noticed. They all seem the same to me.'

'That's why,' I say. 'They are.'

The drummer smacks around his planets like a waiter laying plastic plates upon a table. 'Love me, love me do,' sings the singer.

We should have stayed as nomads, all of us. Our grateful, nurturing beasts, we lead them from the lake, blue water, up to the sky, we're Noahs, sober – up through the sepia rocks, the trail boss leads the song, a song that never changes, infinitely long, always renewed. Each transhumance new – a rock has slipped, a root's laid bare. At night we hammer out our golden crowns and necklaces ...

Here, there's a frozen moment. Krystal leans against me, and the moon – can it appear so large? It seems it can. The tent looks like a grounded airship, and the sign, the 'Krystal Bar', holds steady, and the shadows pale. The guys, the villagers, who rummage through our bins, are caught in frozen frame. The grass is silver spikes, the band sticks upon a chord, the file of officers who stand in line outside – their medals silent now, no chests are pouting and the badges on their caps send out a tiny cymbal 'ting'...

And then she's gone, Krystal ... I hear her say: 'Alan – I need a guy with power whom I can trust. That guy, your mate Jan – he's always wandering off ...' and Alan says, 'It's so. He is my friend, my brother – but it's true, his bones are marked with treachery, right through and through, like sticks of seaside rock.' I tell Shusha, 'We were all frozen then, a moment back. Now, everything is like it is – but smell the peace! Just like it was before ... before the change of partners, everywhere...' She stares at me:

'You're mad,' she says: 'And don't think of taking me away, with milking those woolly cowlike things. Yaks. They're in the movies all the time. And walking miles. It must be lack of sleep with you. I'll talk to Krystal. Maybe we could start a chain of bars, all similar, and have you on a mountain-top, as manager. No villagers that steal your trash. And as for me – we'll see.'

Later, Krystal says, 'We need to keep those villagers in line. Alan and his mates – they say there are intelligent squibs that only burn the trees. They use them where Salm and Ziad used to live.'

And down they go, Alan, his mates, and Krystal too, off to the village. Down go the trees. The villagers still steal our trash. You might have known. 'No reprisals, you guys down there, and our guys too!' says Alan. 'No allegories, no one else's hassles, nothing portentous, universal. It's just us, having a good time. The others too.'

'It's these Central Asians,' Krystal says. 'Sensitive to noise. It's the memory of the steppe. There, only wind.'

'Phew,' Shusha says to me. 'Those orthodox monks – they've an opinion on every goddam thing. Transubstantiation. Root vegetables. Exhausting. Too bad you got the nonsense job. It's that you're not so bright. There's Alan with his soldiers – he's a straight: those colonels – they're all gay, my, how they love his shoulder. Such a comfort! Krystal – doing what she does. Me, in the corner, arguing with drunks.'

I look into her eyes: those uppers Krystal gives, to keep us on our toes – they lodge in Shusha's eyes: they're black all over, I'm staring down the barrels of iron cannons. She says,

'Krystal wants to give the show to locals. She'll keep me – and Alan too. Salm might draw quietly on, his point, his line, gone for a run. But you, my dear ...'

I'm alarmed. I say, 'The guys from here can do the work lots better than we can. Better than Krystal too.'

'Exactly so,' says Shusha. 'It's just that I'm an indispensable. You are not.'

'A strike? On your behalf?' Salm asks me. 'They say some villagers is dead. You may be the guy responsible. Forget a strike – it won't absolve. My cartoons go down well, win sympathy. The clients see the world is churning, they like it drawn in little squares, and funny too.'

'The dead guys,' Alan says, 'they probably did it all themselves. See – those cadavers wearing quite wrong clothes.

But certainly, they need a sacrifice. From us. From you,' he points at me.

'Alan,' I say, 'forget it, my old friend.'

Are you satisfied / With an average life? – as the song says.

'The guys here, they're not like us,' says Krystal. 'They're used to living at the crossroads. People trekking to and fro, all sorts. You'll get a swift fair trial. Local rules. Shusha can defend you. Alan's too close to his military, Salm is set to swell out into murals. Graffiti on the tent. They'll hide the graffiti already on it.' She talks on for a while about her plans.

I say, 'Shusha, maybe I should have examined you more closely – personality, beliefs. I stopped at your face. In awe at the money spent on it.'

'That's just a part of things,' she says. 'Now you want a story to save your neck?'

'No, Shusha, I want that, sure, but also subtle answers to the way things happen.'

'You always come back there,' she says. 'It's your ruination, and over and over ... Intelligence, lovers come, lovers leave, and you think there's an answer? A question?'

'Shusha,' I say, 'be Sheherazade, like you were before I knew you. Save my neck. Draw your eyebrows, to meet in the middle.'

'Even before I met you,' she says, 'I'd got tired of the physical.'

'Just steal from yourself. An opinion. For me. Remember how they stole those old Leadbelly songs, and made their fortunes. I love these Central Asians ...' and she interrupts,

'It's better call them Middle Asians. They've a sharp sense of their future. Salm's already drawn it. Ask him about yourself.'

I'm wearing the wrong clothes. The cadavers are in the middle, and round, the lesser judges. Krystal says, 'These guys are used to being paid or threatened. Or both. So I'll offer nothing – that way justice can be done.'

Shusha tells the head judge her story: 'There was a young guy, in the Delta. He went digging for crabs. There's been a dearth. Instead of crabs, he found a unique disc of Delta blues. He went home, and played it. It was a marvel. Then, he thought of selling to some local group. Instead, he played the disc again. Over and over.' She turns to me: 'It was your mention of Leadbelly ...'

'I guessed that,' I say.

'It's a fantastic story,' says the judge, 'and quite uplifting. But – these cadavers. We have an effect. We should seek a cause.'

'I don't think my friend,' says Susha, pointing at me, 'had much to do with it.' I say,

'Not "friend", Shusha, "client".'

'No, no,' she says, 'that's a cash relationship. You've misread the culture.'

'I've no idea who this guy is,' says the judge, staring at me, 'or you either,' staring at Shusha. 'So how'd I know his part?'

It seems an impasse.

'I expect you're innocent,' says Krystal. 'But you no longer have the protection of the Roof.'

'I dare say you're guilty,' says the judge, 'but we can hardly punish you. These cadavers – we don't know what they'd done, how they got here.'

Shusha says, 'What he means is – the present allows no doubt. The past, the future – they are full of it, but the now is what you see, and what there is. So, you're not guilty, and not innocent. Juxtaposed. Like the guy who found the disc – you look for one thing, and you find another.'

The minor judges seem convinced. Justice has been seen. Not done.

'There!' says Salm. 'You see? It's exactly as Shusha says. I've drawn your future – my little scrawl. Not one thing, nor another. Like Ziad. Material, then – gone, quite immaterial. My "Salm", he's there, movement, but intangible.'

'You see?' Shusha says to me. 'My story saved your neck. You see! – the law is argument, opinion. That is all.'

I say, 'I don't know if I'm guilty, and what for. Those guys, cadavers – accidents? And accident is history, running deep. It's ancestors. Intention is shallow, hits at everyone, quite indiscriminate.'

'I thought Salm was the passenger, that gets sent back,' says Alan, in his friendly way. 'It seems that it was you.' They stare at me.

'Look,' says Shusha, 'do you think it was a trial? The dead all bundled up? Elders? A sentence to infinity? The trouble is, you're a romantic, Jan – especially, it seems, about these guys out here. It's all in Krystal's plan – her idea of drama, like you see on the TV. Motiveless crimes, and quickly find some patsy, who'll play guilt.'

They laugh ... Some guy, some barman, waits in the wings and wants my job.

'It's drama,' Shusha says. 'No one's problem but yours. Burning the forest, killing guys.'

'A drama?' I ask. 'I never heard, I never spoke. As for the trees – not me!'

'Then we could do it all over, without words. I'll be the corpse this time. See, I'm trying to teach you something,' she says.

'It's not something I don't know,' I say.

'No point in teaching you what you don't understand,' she says, briskly. 'Maybe one of those bundles was Ziad. Maybe one was supposed to be you. It's all anonymous.'

'Or Krystal,' I say. 'Her ideas are deadly.'

'No,' she says, 'not Krystal. The drama bleeds off our anger. You can't hate her. Sitting there, sunset to dawn, the sleeplessness, the pills – you're sucked in, and forget. The wind blows over you, the little thistle bushes dance around like dusty trolls. Your fantasy convicts you and absolves.'

'The scene is sharp,' I say. 'Besides, we hardly knew Ziad.'

'It all becomes generic. Another victim. That way you can cope – even if the victim's you.'

'No, Shusha, I don't feel that last bit,' I say.

'Well,' says Shusha, 'maybe we should do it over. New scenario. No words this time.'

I say, 'I just want to pour those drinks.'

'That is your problem,' Shusha says. 'Wanting rubbishy stuff. A cuddle and a rut, a binge. No majesty. Think tribal chiefs, think dead queens in golden boxes. Think yourself up, off your knees.'

There's Salm. Up his ladder, with a laser pen, he draws upon the canvas. The tent's already smeared with writings, words forgotten instantly, big globs of paint, thin legs of stuff – acryllic, could it be? – leak down and stop, standing on the intermediate.

'This fucking light won't stick,' Salm shouts. He draws and draws, the light's a frantic line.

'On, on,' shrieks Krystal. 'Everybody! Come and watch!'

And so they do, the guys with guns, the guys with plastic badges on their hats, on their lapels, the guys with slogans on their shirts, the drunk, the less drunk, and the drying out ...

'Krystal!' shouts Salm, 'I cannot make a mark,' and Krystal shouts back, 'Do it for the crowd, dear Salm.'

He scrabbles now, uses the whole expanse of canvas, on and on the little point of light proceeds, an epic intricate, heroes on elephants, no doubt; rivers to swim, and oceans too, and demons with expensive masks, lovers on palanquins, on reed beds, and on clouds...A moral too, for sure, loyalty, obsession, mountains to climb, the bad to kill with magic arrows, a wedding, at the last.

Some guys cheer, and others sleep upon the grass.

I'm with the villagers. They don't care, and I've nothing for them. Not even a word in the language.

I say to Krystal, 'Those trees, the forests ... apples. Ur-apples. The trees you burnt. They're the origin, our first apples, and the bears select, and eat, and crap the best, the seeds, the noble hybrids...'

'Yes, yes,' she says. 'Hallucinate – that's the best part of no sleep: no dream.'

'No, no,' I say. 'The trees of beauty, magnificence. That's knowledge, the best part of it. Abounding – you didn't burn them all?'

'I don't expect so,' Krystal says. 'Those guys resisted. Wow!'

Salm says, 'We used to have fruit trees, but you need a place to put the suburbs.'

'Peaches and cream – like your cranes and egrets, I dare say,' says Krystal, disrespectful to the living and the probable dead. 'Just draw, Salm, don't talk and break the flow. My flow.'

Shusha says, 'Krystal, dear leader, tell your scheme,' and Krystal says, 'we have the cash to pay our debt, to buy the tent, and everything. But—' she winks '—perhaps we'll do a flit.'

We strike the tent. It's always night, the tiny moon is laser-bright, the trees are thick with learned apples, maybe they glint like pearls. We flit in silence, and the animals are complicit, they let off no neigh or bray. It is a frozen moment. We steal away. We leave the bundled dead. We leave our guilt, and justice, truth, and all the rest. We leave the band.

'Goddam Light Cavalry,' Krystal says. 'A thousand miles of it, always at the Charge,' and Alan laughs, although the band has been his choice, and says, 'Light Calvary', but we don't care, we're nomads, finally.

It is my destiny. The frozen moment lodges in my brain, a glacier, it penetrates a fold, then doesn't move. 'Nomads, at last,' I say to Shusha, with delight.

'You always were,' she says.

The walking doesn't suit. The riding hurts still more.

Higher and higher.

We shall all die, quite differently from what we feared.

'Those sheep,' says Shusha, 'staring at us. Devil's horns, of finest bronze.'

Salm says, 'This is a surprise ... ending here. I thought it would have been in my street, or some small space.'

It's brown, then grey, then white: 'On and up,' shouts Krystal, and to me she gasps, 'Maybe we should leave Alan here – prophet among the rocks. Keeping away from all the rest. Keeping the rest away from us.'

It is a kind of march, no arms or uniforms. We are here to remember our dead, our comrades. We are here because we stole the tent.

This is all there is to being nomads – this, except for the happiness, the singing, and the larger lungs.

'We find three trees, we set our tent on them,' says Krystal. 'With all this space, these gangs – only invented apples! Left distribution to the bears. It's hardly much.'

There's no trees here. We cuddle down. There is no band, but bands will come and play wherever there are one or two with nothing else to do but listen, wave their arms – a band would set up on the moon, just need a system loud enough to boom to earth.

'Love?' asks Shusha. 'Doesn't enter in. It's doing something someone else desires. A heavy body, visiting your bed, and then it's up to you to bury it.'

The other nomads that we see light fires at night. Krystal's afraid of bears, we sleep beneath the pinhole of the moon, we call it dark, instead, it's light transforming. Alan alone sleeps in the cold, the rest of us pair up, and hug.

'No past,' says Shusha. 'Just us. It's better so. Just our desires, and all the rest is circumstance, come beating on our door. Not yours, of course, not yet. And – no doors here.'

I ask, 'What desires can you, can anyone, have, with Krystal driving us?'

Shusha says, 'Just a fire.'

'Alan is poison,' I say: it's an old obsession of mine.

'Only to himself,' says Shusha. 'Besides, neither of us cares about him. He's just a friend.'

'Well,' I say, 'I've been honest about him, and me. Nevertheless, we shouldn't leave him here.'

'Krystal had no plan for that,' says Shusha. 'He's not the one that gets left. Maybe no one's left this time around.'

Salm's uncle – he'd have taken apple seeds from here, carted them home. Salm has his ancestors, even though they don't impinge. What a comedown – last of the family, invent a character, a line – like early Korky Kat. An artist, nothing more. No glass, no caravans.

'Krystal protects us,' Shusha says, although there is no threat, except the cold.

'I've found the cold I need!' says Alan, 'though now it doesn't fit the Mass. Down in the valley, they'll have found their way, with everyone on chariots, driven by the sun. The sun! That should be my faith ...'

'There's sun here too, Alan, cool and pale. The animals have wandered off, with everything,' says Salm. 'Here, there's nothing you can tie them to.'

'Another plan!' shouts Krystal. 'I've got it. And are we far from Apple City, anyone?'

'I'm not walking all that way,' says Shusha. 'That's fact, not an opinion, guys.'

A fresh solution

'We're refugees,' says Krystal to the guy. 'Minister', his badge says.

'We're artists,' Shusha adds. 'We've lost some canvas, with graffiti.'

'You don't look like artists, or refugees,' says the minister. 'Graffiti belong to everyone. There is no lost and found. Besides – what are you fleeing from? What do you expect to find.'

'We're fleeing from lots,' says Krystal. 'Wrong beliefs, wrong neighbours. No beliefs, the wrong kind of God. Salm here – is known all over. Syria, Iran – they love him.'

'Hmmm,' says the minister. 'I wonder if you're in the right place?'

Alan says to me, 'I told you so. Thoughts are always welcome, bodies never.'

'We can brighten everything,' says Shusha. 'Stories! Keep you awake all night. Make you postpone the executions.'

'Sing me a song,' says the minister. 'If it catches, I might let you in.'

'Apples,' says Alan. 'There's an old one by Cream – "atonal apples and petrified heat" comes in,' and he hums it.

'Don't fuss so, Alan,' says Krystal. '"Looking for the golden light" will do as well. It's Beethoven, an anthem.'

'International,' says the minister, chanting along: '"Wagt es zu denken". Everyone knows it, from the contest.'

'The Krystal Bar, that was our star,' I say. 'The Roof – stand on it and see as far as you can bear. Shelter under it. We're neither left nor right, neither believers nor the lapsed.'

'Well,' says the guy. 'That makes a difficulty. Neither uplift nor subversion. Just voyaging. Not seeing much. Committing crimes – and then excusing them.'

'Unfortunately,' says Krystal, 'these guys that work for me are quite reactionary, from living in some backward spots.'

'Well, welcome then,' the guy says: minister – a stereotype. 'Come on, join us here. Just don't step out of line. Again.'

He leaves the room. 'Where's he gone?' asks Alan. 'To get our passports?'

'Maybe,' says Krystal. 'But if they're so keen on us, they might not let us leave ...'

We run out – not instinct, but science, and the empirical, our driver now. The streets – enormous here, the statues plentiful and huge – each daring figure holds a shiny golden fruit. Wisdom, good and evil – there's everything. We run away.

'Maybe Salm should be left,' says Shusha. 'Here, as an artist, if you're good, you're chivvied, if you're bad, you're feted. Either way, it's fame.'

'No, no,' says Krystal. 'He is our badge. It's true, I haven't time to follow what he does. It's genius for sure. And if you say it's crap, he'll take it badly, sulk for days. No, no, we keep him – otherwise, we're merely running bars, with nothing chic. Just let him draw his comics – one day, he will disappear into his creation, like a god. Disappear like Ziad. Self-immolation – that's what drawing's all about – see, it's the picture you remember, not the guy who did it. That guy's not around. Wanting his immortality, or at least a celebrated life, Salm will pass into the charcoal "Salm". And that will be the end to it. Then,' she laughs lightly, 'I get the rights.'

Home

'Well,' asks Krystal, 'What did this all mean to you, Alan?'

'I sought, I learned a little. Not a lot. Here I am, safe in my skin,' he says.

'Hmm,' says Krystal, 'ungrateful. Still clinging to an inner life? I don't see the use of one myself. Shusha?'

'Were we part of the struggle or the flight?' Shusha asks. 'Certainly, I talked a lot. Always on the right side.'

Krystal says I don't fall in a category, so it doesn't seem I count for much.

Salm says, 'I guess Ziad's somewhere, or he's not. Me – up to my neck in history.'

Shusha says, 'Our hopes were illusion. Those stories – pass the night, another day comes, you try to sleep, and find some cash. There ought to be a word "to sheherazade" – while the time away, avoid the executioner.'

I say, 'There's apples everywhere, but the forest's been dug up, burnt, cut down ... The roots ...'

'That's crap,' says Krystal briskly. 'Forget the roots, that's quite reactionary. Think "better apples". Experiment. Means, not ends. The end's been written, anyway – it's not good.'

I tell Phil, the unemployed novelist, my friend: 'Krystal says I don't fit in a category.'

'She's kind,' he says. 'You sure do fit. Lots. A spy. For the Americans, too. Then – a renegade at least twice over. And Alan? His tunes?'

'Small ideas. Commissions. That is all it takes.'

He asks, 'Shusha?'

'Opinions never end. Especially about those close to her.'

I add, 'Krystal's a slaver. It is all for art. That's all that's left – we wandered through the ruins. Sometimes, they may have been new starts.'

He says, 'There's lots been burnt, by nature, or by your kind of guy. The scientists – they're good at measuring what's left.' He laughs. 'Salm's country's settled down. You read him in the paper every week. His mascot, Mickey Mouse, or something like – he's wry ... It fits the situation.'

He offers me a job. He doesn't write, he earns. I say, 'This job. Not pouring drinks?'

He says, 'Finding a woman. I met her on a train – it's a branch line. It should be easy for you. She came from Leningrad. It wasn't called so by then, of course.'

'More fun for you to do the search.'

'No time. A real search, mind,' says Phil. 'On foot.'

'What did she say?' I ask.

'I commiserated with her, on how her country had slid down. We seem to commiserate a lot like that,' he says, 'with everyone.'

'I don't hold with countries,' I say.

'In her case,' he says, 'that's especially unnecessary.'

'You must be earning well, to pay for this,' I say.

Phil strikes a stance: 'She said – "we're down. That's not all bad. But you will go down too, and keep on going down, and struggling and going down, until you disappear. It's worse for you, because you'd no belief to lose. Faith makes one strong, and losing faith – it makes you stronger still."'

It seems quite unremarkable: I say, 'Unless she was religious, faith in that context sounds a little strained.'

'That's what I want to know,' says Phil. 'Exactly what was lost. And what we'll lose. She said, "You'll disappear. Falling off the page. It can't be painless. Like those armies lost beneath the sand – the soldiers – all the males, gone and so everything no more."'

'This "you",' I say, 'she meant your world, your people, not just "Phil". There's no panic, though. It's physics – lost particles attach to other clusters. Nothing's thrown away.'

'Well,' says Phil, 'she convinced me, and she's right. All the other people that you know, gone, like falling off a raft ...'

'She was beautiful too,' I say.

'I don't remember. It doesn't signify. She said, "You're a good man, Philip. It's all a pity."'

'That's always good to hear,' I say.

He says, 'Ruin. A good man. That's what she said. Find her.'

That was easy. Here's her house. Someone's practising contralto sax. I hope it's not her kid.

She's alone. I see no sax. Can she have hidden it? I explain things.

'He could have come himself,' says Nikki. 'Although I don't see why.'

'He likes things bone-clean,' I say. 'There was talk of belief, of faith. I guess he wanted you to be quite clinical about it.'

'The collapse, the disappearance, I was right,' she says. She has cat's cheeks, cat's eyes. She stands there, in her nice body.

'I guess,' I say. 'Everyone says so. I'm not the boss – it all seems bad to me, but I'm not high up enough for optimism.'

'I learnt to think of things forever getting better. And now I know they don't,' she says.

It's all a disappointment. I feel I'm poncing for my friend.

'Didn't I hear a sax?' I say.

'I'm in a band – they used to say a "girl band", now they don't,' she says. The room is quite bare – music must be what she does. I linger. Her power, her sexual power – it's like a fire, set in the middle of the floor.

'That's all I have to say,' she says. 'Don't worry, the ones who come after, they will dig us up, and speculate.'

'The bodies chipped and charred,' I say. 'Don't you have any more to say?'

Shusha – she always has some more.

'No,' says Nikki. 'And – you can't dig up the thoughts.'

I'm waiting for her to tell me I'm a good man too.

'I must get on with studying,' she says.

'OK, that's it,' says Phil, when I get back. 'Here's for your trouble.'

'Is that all I get?' I ask.

'You said finding her was easy. Little pay for little graft.'

Phil was the brightest of us all.

'And shall you go and see her?' I ask.

'I think not, if that was all she had to say. That's why it had to be you who went. She just repeats.'

'It seems a waste,' I say. 'Of her, not you.'

'If I'm without a job again, I'll maybe put her in a book. White witch,' Phil says.

'What is your famous job?' I ask.

'I consult – on places far away, you've never heard of them,' he says. 'Even on Nikki's origins, though not much interested there.'

'I bet I've been to where you mean,' I say. 'We saw the apple trees.'

'Science is helping there, once they had burnt the whole lot down,' he says, with quiet authority.

Later, I go to Krystal. 'Anything for me?' I ask.

'Of course,' she says. 'I don't forget my slaves. The deal is this. You know the States? There were disasters, one, two, three, and more, and then the Mexicans and all the rest – fought to take it over, where all their people were. Now, places like New York – there's wastes. People wandering round, with no identity. For us – still culture, that's the theme. A bookstore. Without books – we show some pages on a screen. Of course, now, there's music behind everything. That's for Alan. You – the drinks again, but there is scope for fantasy. That way the clients pay for what they see, and when they've drunk, they pay again for what we tell them that they saw. Shusha – will do her TV show, host all that talk and add her two centsworth.'

'I didn't know about Shusha, and her work,' I say.

'Poor girl,' says Krystal. 'She is my best friend, but quite lacks personality. That's what they want, it seems. People are disoriented, need to talk it out, what they all were, and so, and so. Some tears. Of course, the Yanks are loud and rather shits, but – we shall hold our nose, hold out our hands!'

'What structure will we do it in?' I ask.

'No tent,' she says. 'A structure like they used to sell the snake-oil and elixirs in, when their world was young and they just fought among themselves.'

'That structure is a tent,' I say.

'Well, be it so,' she says. 'I'm disappointed in poor Salm. He made it big, and where he's from, it means that he could disappear. He's gone, he left me ... Made it big. Cartoons and comics. Just imagine!'

For us, ghost books for ghosts. I say to Alan, 'There's a solo sax player that I know, available ...'

'Oh yes? Hmmm,' he says.

'I didn't know you'd broken through,' I say to Shusha.

'You'd have found out in time. Besides, you're not my agent. All us Arabs in exile – there's a public. Where'd we go? It's a good theme.'

Later:

Krystal doesn't let us sleep, but when a page is on the wall, we get a break.

There's this old guy – he wears his skullcap, but I don't know exactly where he's from, which clan.

'Resist, resist, you apples! Come on you...!' he shouts. During my breaks, we're in his laboratory, and it's full of apple pieces, seeds and roots. The guy says I can be a scientist, even the saviour of the world. He'll teach me. Of course, that may all be snake-oil, or a story like those Shusha told.

We must invent again the fathers of all apples, the strain original – and then re-create those forests burnt, the source of all our apples, wisdom, evil, wealth.

I splice the apple bits together: 'Come on, you little fuckers, stick,' I shout, and he shouts too, 'Resist, resist.'

Lola

'Pips! Pips! You clod!' The old guy, scientist, world saviour on the brink ... he throws some pulp, and cuffs me, roars, 'Stick 'em right in!'

This is not the way. Things burnt, the cities falling down. You hear the trucks, the heavy-booted guys leap off, run down your street. Poor Nikki, found, before she's lost again. Subsistence, deference – that's not at all the way.

'Enough! Enough of science. And of fruit,' I shout. I slam the door, I see my old Kazakh, mouth like an *omul''*s, gasping behind the deep deep glass.

At last! Down with manipulation, with Krystal – the great deceiver – with stories and fantasies, Shusha too, she with the eyebrows and no personality. How we love manipulation: done to us – see how far they'll dare to go! – everything is being tweaked by someone or the whole design; the circumstance, the earthquake, supreme clockfixers, dragging us along to old age and the grave.

I have lacked nobility, a scale of excellence to climb. Remember that trumpeter, when he got bored with people, he walked out. Looking for a fix. Not leaving his public: just his family, all those kids. Chet, his name: great voice. 'How could you know what love is?' he sang. What a take ...

I walk out on Krystal and that gang. I think: Jerusalem had seven gates, but other, more forgotten cities, more splendid, had a hundred, each with a battalion, ready for the sally. Enemies all round. I must get some enemies, and some exits, forever defended, prickly too. At last, I've found the key, my purpose, the end of all of it. What to wear and drink along the way, where to stay, and who to say I know. Is anyone interested?

'*Is anyone* ...' I shout. Being a scientist was rubbish. Poking bits of this and that together, squinting down glass tubes that cost a lot. Come on guys! We've all to meet our maker, don't complain – what can we say? 'Hi, I'm broken: Maker, make me another me?'

'Bubbling along, I see?'

Oh no, it's that guy, frequenter of the culture tent. Here everyone has names that don't give clues to origins. What's this one? A Stanis? Miles? A Woody? He's drunk deep of our pages, lit up on the wall; he's tanned – that means he's from a South; or unemployed, with time to lie beneath an artificial sun. 'You must remember me?' he says, 'I'm Chet! You've seen me in your dreadful show.'

'Of course,' I tell a half untruth. 'I was just considering you – at least, your namesake. Chet Baker, naturally, born a trumpeter discreet. Forget you saw me once before – I've changed my life, my destiny, since then.'

'That sounds pretentious – but, of course,' he says, 'you don't believe in reincarnation, so you change your life, over and over – like a fox that dumps its fleas, you swim out in the flow, and all the parasites jump off and drown. But – friend – it isn't so. Those ticks are bolted on. Don't trust the river – take the golden stair, and higher, higher, till you're sucking in ... great draughts of heaven—'

I interrupt. 'I've tried all that, dear Chet – up on the mountain, your animals run off, you go down, you seek the city, wandering up and down along, statues and streets, the offices and cops, the ruins, all that stuff—'

He cuts me short. 'You're a good egg, Jan. It is Jan, no? But you're a blown egg, empty, ready to be filled.'

I hear his call, a flourish. Might be Bruckner, and those sweet brown cows, milk tasting of fresh calvados.

'No cows,' says Chet firmly. 'And bulls on the roof, not under it.'

'I want to be on the winning side,' I say.

All around, there's graffiti, moving. Some like targets. How'd they do it? Sliding on the wall and round the corner. Salm – his signature. It's like the sea, on and on, quite inconclusive. Wine-dark, to drinkers. A void, quite airless, if you can't swim. Waves round the corners – are they going anywhere, or just responding to the force beneath? the Niebelungen ...

Chet interrupts, 'Nothing is as you say, your women, and your handle on the universe, all your thought was wrong; that all went down, but all the rest, reality, it stayed the same and still. Frozen centuries. Winning? Then forget the poor, class war, gender, and frolics generally. Those are the best for sure – justice and truth lie there within, encysted. Forget all that. You'll lose. Remember, if you win, there's lots of carrion guys will want to be there too, so you'd need to hold your nose, when you hold out your hand ... Don't sell your soul, that market's saturate!'

We tour New York, we ride on an electric chariot. I say, 'There is the subway we could take ...' but he says the tunnel's fallen in, the wires and pipes beneath are blocked, like entrails terminal ... There's the museum, where the modern art becomes the postcards that we used to send. There's poor guys up and down, and muttering, an automobile or two, and lots of empty spaces, sheds that smell of mothkill, waterways that's green and red and orange too. It takes an hour, we're back.

'Here,' says Chet, 'we'll eat a fried-egg sandwich, best in town. The chickens never stop, they'll never fail until the galaxy collides, and falls into Andromeda ...' Then,

'A ride?' asks Chet, 'as when I'm clean, it gives a sense, perspective ...'

Here's the funfair, we're the only ones. We're tied tight in, the car's a chicken, and Chet says seize coincidence, it's maybe all you'll find, and we are off, our heads spin round like nebulae, the ride is up and down, so quick we see the past, those primal Irish gangs, the future too – the gangs are Kazakhs now, and 'Nature's gentlemen', says Chet, and winks and rubs his nose – and nearly falls. There are the oceans; over there – the pigs and chickens; up there's snow, and down there's peppers, maize like forged bronze finials, guys in hats, and trenches dug to stop the Mexicans, and ...

'Well,' says Chet, 'that's it. That is the States. There's people come from everywhere – there's guides that show the ruins too, these chariot affairs, or there are carts with llamas ...' on he goes.

'Chet,' I say, 'I know all this. Where does it lead?'

'Lead, Jan?' he says, and maybe sheds a tear: 'Not leads. It led. And now, it's up to you.'

I cheer him up. 'Those bold young sycamores, in the pavement cracks, sign of something new.'

'Yes,' he says. 'We'll rise again – as forest maybe, and all will live in trees. That's where we started, where we should be at the end. Tree houses. And – that Wall Street, should be Wool Street, you should see the sheep ...'

'I'd heard about that, Chet,' I say. 'But where do I come in?'

'I've been catching up on literature,' he says. 'And after. But here, well, – when it's over, it is over. And weren't those fried egg sandwiches just the best?'

'There must be more,' I say, not knowing. Maybe a rebirth's on the way.

'Moscow has lots of space,' says Chet. 'They're the best at circuses. But yes, I remember lilac here, and acacia. Parades of guys who looked like Henry James.'

'How about the Bowl games, and sleeping on the sidewalk after?' I ask, trying to cheer him.

'Nah,' says Chet, 'I never went for sports.'

His mission, and his origins? He says, 'The suburbs – that writer said that's where the angels live, when they're called out, they grow to thirty metres tall, and whoosh! like rockets, up they go. The heavenly hosts. And every one comes back.'

'Yes, Chet, but you? Abused when young, a gang and jail? Or quite the other way – white ponies and some sexy maids?'

He looks at me, disappointed. 'I never knew,' he says. 'You thought in stereotypes and settling scores.'

'Oh yes,' I say. 'It cuts things short.'

'When you went up that mountain top,' he asks, 'you must have felt the spirit closing in?'

'Of course,' I say, 'the cold. The absence. Then the presence, warming up.'

'It sounds,' he says, 'like what the *Bhagavad Gita* says, about the cold. In Buddhism—'

'Yes, yes,' I say. 'We did it all in school.'

'Oh, so did we,' he says, 'but it doesn't stick to everyone. Imagine – Yanks elect a Buddhist president – so, bang! a military coup!'

'That's true quite everywhere,' I say, and think of Alan and his chilly Mass. 'In outer space, it's cold as hell, they say – but think of all those stars, and Roman candles spurting up. What spectacles.' We ponder, silently. Together, we have reached a boundary.

'Look, Chet,' I say. 'I don't know what you have in mind. But treks and marches, golden light – no, no! I want my five per cent, or even more.'

'OK,' he says, 'so you're like that. I didn't know. It's hard to fathom other people deep inside.'

'If that is what you want,' I say, 'it's so.'

'I'll tell you, Jan,' he says, pushing his canny coppery face an inch from mine, 'I have been known to walk out too. It's a genetic thing. You get it from your namesake, through your Ma.'

'I don't want to be a celebrity,' I say. 'I've lived through all that.'

'No difficulty,' Chet says, 'all us survivors are celebrities. Besides, you haven't the physique. Forget it – forget politics, your past's against it. Either you killed them, when you spied, or else they got away, and now sit firm on crystal thrones. You're poison, Jan, and that's your blessing – the innocent – that's what they always say – are gunned down and their hands cut off, and thrust into some orifice. You're just poison, people run from you. That's a great gift.'

'I hadn't seen,' I say, quite gratified. 'I just poured drinks.'

'You got off that murder rap ... The other spies, hived off in that porno band, are cinders now. The nasty ones – come to the top when all the patsies try and fall. Now, you're at the top. It's true, there isn't much beneath, but – whaddya want, a factory job, some place in Xinjiang?' He stumbles over the word, the place – it's clear, it's just a ghost word for him, a place where only ghosts track on.

'The thing is this,' Chet insists, 'the strong fall down, as do the weak. Some guys get up, and others leach out in the sand. Our little group's equipped for both – for rise, for fall.'

I consider this. 'Maybe behind the bar's my destiny,' I say, and Chet applauds, in silence. 'Yes! Reluctance. Waiting for the auspice! That's the way.'

Where does this lead?

'"The noisy kids, they broke their big toy," that's what Lola thinks,' says Chet. '"The wars were fought, they didn't mend the toy. Capitalists!"'

'Who's Lola?' I ask.

'Hey, guy!' says Chet. 'You haven't turned a buck for us! Go get.'

There is a gang that cleans up neighbourhoods. It pays. It's us.

Krystal's the only person with some cash, at least, the only one I know.

'You renegade,' she says. 'Although – the new guy mixes drinks superb. We've no regrets.'

I say, 'Look, Krystal – I work now for some other guys, and I can help. We have the long view – rise or fall may come, the modest life, or excess – what's good, what's bad, you have to hedge along ...'

She's not inviting.

I say, 'We can clean things up for you. The bookstore up the street, competing – that should not be there. This tent of yours – without a permit – it's ephemeral. The guys that doze along the sidewalk – we could move those right along ...' and on I talk, it comes quite natural.

'OK,' she says, 'I grasp your business. Fix the lot, and quick. How much?'

We never fix her competition, they persuade us – but the rest is done.

'Now,' says Chet with pride, 'you'll see Lola,' and – there she is. She lounges, like a mountain lion, an ancient book is by her side. She writes, she thinks, her golden hair foams like the tide – soft shoulders, she is all rounded, face – a slight pucker with invention ... She wears a kind of sari, badly tied, a pomegranate red, with silver scrolls.

'Fuck off, Chet,' she says, 'I've nearly worked this out.' We stand in silence, then she says, 'You see, you play the little numbers, maybe one or two, the ones that don't turn up, you shift from wheel to wheel, you win a little – then, one day, you bet the lot. You win a fortune, or you lose – but if you lose, you're ruined, if you win, you make a sacrifice – of everything...' on she talks,

'Those wooden cities, burnt, a sacrifice, collective suicide, the golden crowns that weigh ten kilos – who could wear them? – amber seals ... And then they burn the city down, leap in the fire. No tombs, just ash and charcoal. Or, there's Asmavedha – the most lovely horse is petted for how long? – and then gets sacrificed. Bayram. Isaac. That way, you lose a sheep.' She rambles on, she turns the keys of life in rusty locks, lists out the secrets, never finds the clue that violates their mystery.

'Help me out, you guys,' she says. 'It seems it always happens – things are going well – and then, in gratitude, the system's thrown into the fire ... Genetics function – oh no! the most prized beast is butchered up. Or else – things go badly – so we do the same, the best things thrown away...No rain? No problem, poison the well, the gods will know we love them and have faith in providence ...'

I ask Chet in a whisper, 'This Lola – she's the thinking part of you. Is this her best? The death wish?' Lola turns a page, oblivious. Chet whispers back, 'This is the best that we could find. It makes a kind of sense. Things went so well with us, but then the guys in charge, who knew the mechanisms – they screwed it up. It all fell down.'

Lola says, 'What you animals back there – what you whispering about? Come on, you, the new one. I hate this "me", being a pro thinker – time for someone new ... sing us your song!'

There's a lot of nose and jaw in what Lola says, it drags things out, it makes you patient. For hand, she says 'heeand'.

'Come on!' she says to me. 'You, the poison tree – I smell your smell from here.'

I tell her about intelligence: the apples and their science, and how you have to travel to find the meagrest mystery. 'Music runs through it,' I say, and think of Alan, how he said, 'This religious stuff – what makes it difficult to write it out is having this pebble in your mouth. More than a pebble – a rock, a sharp red rock. Disbelief.'

'Lola,' I say, 'what's important is not the negativity in things, it's what's unique – not just the *omul'*, but his brother – that's even more unique.' I stumble, just like Chet in Xinjiang: 'Some aspects of quite natural things – the moon when tiny, a glint – though of course, it's not been there for ever, not from the start, not at the end.'

'Hmm,' says Lola. 'Are you sure you're the sophisticate Chet promised me?'

She thinks a while, then says, 'Well, tuck my end.'

I say, 'I know all about saris,' but this one doesn't seem to have an end. I'm losing challenges. I wrestle with her garment, and she watches me with sea-blue eyes. I think of Julie, and the alp, her sky, her blue.

I ask Lola to a restaurant, but Chet comes too. He's jerking, as if his battery's old. I tell the waiter – 'It shall be ethnic, naturally, but I can't bother with these numbers on the menu, and the stuff is complex.'

'So,' he says. 'Just "Treats", OK?'

'But nothing live,' I say.

He writes 'Dead Treats'.

Later, Lola, poking at a toad, says, 'I don't go lots for food.'

I pay with cash I skimmed off what Krystal paid to be protected. As we leave, I see Chet's shirt which says, 'Gift of the people ...' He turns and says, 'I guess it's ethnic, sitting on the floor like that – it makes your stomach curl up tight and close ...' I feel this is my worst shot yet ... this crew ... even the Krystal Bar was good, compared.

'Don't get us wrong,' says Lola, tucking folds of cloth: 'This here is not the future – just a bit that those head guys have given up on. Out of here, it's all the same. The bits that's fallen down – they say they will rebuild. It's just that us – they have no vision for us, so we should be moving on, under our own steam...' Steam. That was a great invention.

On the walls – I guess it was a warehouse – there's some pics, like they were torn from books – a Marx, an Emerson, I see.

'They were all right,' says Chet, with sadness, 'about it all. But so what?' A sign says, 'The Next Move', and Lola says,

'That's us. We're looking for it. But like Engels said, "Too many sects. And not enough movement." Us – we're just a sect...' I interrupt,

'Oh no! I've not fallen in an ashram?'

'No, no,' Lola says. 'We've yet to take a path, or find one – but we shall. The great illusion is to think that what you're on is leading somewhere, or that someone's gone before, and even beaten down the grass and scared the snakes.' She pauses. 'And the toads.'

Guys drop in and out. 'No sex, no dope,' says Lola, reading books. 'We're clean as Persil makes us, here. Clean for whatever journey, clean your underwear, if there's an accident ...'

Now, this looks more promising, this girl, this woman, Marina, loitering here. 'I'm just street trash,' Marina says.

'When it crumbled here,' I say, 'it surely was a terrible thing.'

'No, no,' she says, 'when you know that it goes on – being quite terrible, it's a relief. You swing with it, the rhythm. So long as they don't take you – resettlement. That's the thing it's called ... The gates fell in here, the trumpeters fell off the walls...'

'What gates? What walls?' I ask.

'Cities all had them,' Marina says, a little vague, 'and trumpeters. That is the must.'

'Listen! Listen, all you guys,' shouts Lola. 'What I've come up with. All cases now are exceptional – and so, there's no imperative, categorical or otherwise, no general laws. And – there is no general interest, no universal welfare: we're in warring states. That shows I'm right: – no dope, it screws the brain. No sex – I don't want avid types hanging round our comrades here.'

'There,' says Marina, quite impressed. 'I told you, reading books and thinking on – Lola comes up with vintage stuff.'

I'm impulsive. It's a fault, although they say that it informed the Baroque ... that counts for something. So I say, 'Marina – if this were an old story, you could be a princess, hidden in grime – at least the duke's child, handed over to woodcutters.'

'If that's a compliment,' she says, 'it would be a very old story. I can't sing. So, no: I can't get off the bottom.'

'Dance a little?' I ask.

'No, I teeter. Parents were trailer trash. The pope said I shouldn't be aborted.'

'There you are then,' I say. 'You've got a big name on your side.'

'Not really,' says Marina. 'I'm Marina. Catholics seek land. I'm for the sea. I just head out.'

'That's the best,' I say. She's quick with the riposte, her clothes were once expensive. It's legend that we're all stuck down here, heads maybe only two metres vertical, above the sidewalk. We can shoot upwards, all of us. It is just circumstance. Besides, if Lola has it wrong, we all have the same imperative, part of the same welfare; call it happiness. All under the same Roof. Me on it! I tell Marina all about that. It makes us bond.

I ask, 'What keeps this shed – the Next Move – on the wave? On a track?'

'That's insignificant, banal,' Marina says. 'You were in Intelligence, so you should know. If you can't master simple things, there is a remedy. Study, read a book. Lola confers degrees, if you're interested, and if she thinks you're worth it.

Chet studied, got his laurel wreath, and peaked. It doesn't last, you see. Being clever.' I say,

'Laugh at me, Marina, if you must. It signifies to me, how we work and eat.'

'You chase the hoboes off the sidewalk. You keep order, take the cash from Krystal, and give it to us, we who need it more. There. That's simple, surely. It's like a little country here. Maybe buy some ammunition – if the cops want us for Settlement, we resist. But that's a secret.'

I say, 'This honour that you get – might we be interested?'

Marina says, 'I'm good at other things. It's Greek philosophy. You argue out with Lola. If she wins, you get the wreath. It doesn't matter much – if you fail, next day you do it all again – and you may pass. Maybe some time she'll do the economics, too.'

'It's honour, all the same. A wreath, and you're alive to put it on your head,' I say, impressed.

'I quite give up on you,' Marina says, 'though all this makes you seem quite human, ordinary.'

Lola says to me, 'You know, you're not yet clean. In fact, you've not begun. Your friend Alan – and his Mass: it's used by armies now, it pumps them up. For torture too, I bet. And you! You've still the marks, of working with Intelligence ...'

'No, no,' I say. 'That piece by Alan's not a Mass. It's called the Filles du Calvaire. A station on the Métro. Though of course – it's frightening enough. It pumps you up. And yes, it could be torture, hearing more than once ...'

'You've dodged again,' says Lola. 'Alan's not here. It's you, your inner life was stoppered up. So young, and yet so many twists and wounds.'

'Nothing wrong with curiosity,' says Chet, 'but if your spy lists got it right, then everyone who figured on them – they ended zapped. It was the exceptions made you want to add intelligence to curiosity – but your focus was malign.'

'Remember at dinner,' Lola says, 'how we talked of cities – how the old ones lay around a square. You sit there, on a side, and look across the space. Square – space. And on the other side are guys like you, like in a mirror, looking back. You could be over there, and looking back through space – at you. The answer is to have a cylinder – you'd say it was "in the middle", but of what? Of space! On the cylinder you set the bars, the stores, and when you sit and stare – there's space, quite empty. You don't see other guys, you don't see you, or anyone that's like ...'

'Yes, Lola,' says Marina, 'that's the answer, but what to? Now, take the sea,' and Lola says,

'Yes, yes, Marina!' And to us, 'Marina's speciality's the sea. She has a pirate ship. She is a pirate ship.'

'I'm sea, not ships,' Marina says, 'the sea – is neither space, nor square. It accommodates to any shape of land. At dusk, it's brown, and sometimes grey or black, or blue.'

'You're right, Marina,' Lola says. 'You're on to something there: a thing not bodily, but full of lives; not any kind of form ... We need to ship that thought, and somehow make it work for where we want to be ...'

'Ships ...' says Chet dreamily, 'makes you think of China...'

We are silent: 'Ah, China,' we think, 'if only ...' like our ancestors, thinking, 'Ah, Ellis Island...'

'Jan,' says Lola, 'you did terrible things – for money too, not honour, not glory. Fingering those guys you didn't know. Not much golden light behind your screen ...'

150

'I plead ignorance,' I say, ashamed, found out.

'Just plead,' says Lola. 'Who knows who to.'

I look at Marina, those eyes, like brown agates, polished, in the queen of Egypt's mask. Better be born trash than work to be just trash, for money too, all gone.

'There's all the time to talk,' says Chet. 'If you like talk, it's paradise, and what laws there are, they're Lola's. I don't fancy making them, myself, and seeing what happens to them. "From each ..." is what I say. But it's not like we grow figs, and there's a basketful "from each...". It's like it was before, only tougher. From each is what you take from guys with lots. Or else – you're the each it all gets taken from.'

'When things get better, there'll be more,' Marina says.

'It's what you do when there gets less,' I say. I don't know what.

'Anyway, what's done here isn't protection,' says Marina. 'There's no protection, you don't offer it. It's taking from people with something to take.'

'That sounds improbably easy,' I say. 'Take poor Alan, he'll be working twice as hard: getting other people to work twice as hard.'

'That's all too easy too,' says Lola. 'What you call work, and what I call cash. And I don't make laws, just select a few.'

'Those are your stories, Lola,' Marina says. She and Chet know such things, people's stories, and what's real in them, though in adversity, prying into inner lives isn't worth the time. Everyone is bumming, mostly. Though, when you think, Shusha talked, shouted, raged, waged philosophy – but there was someone else inside, that she spoke to in a different tone. That's where she escaped from me, and escaped to be alone, the two of her. But on the mountain, you couldn't tell, we hugged for warmth, felt good, and anyway, so what?

It's great here, talking – even when Lola says, distributing some brooms, 'Right – empiricists do it better – sweep the shed. Intuitionists can finish up.'

Then, Chet takes me aside. 'If you feel you must persist – your story with Marina. You should avoid their giving you a kicking. Say you're a violinist – that way they'll only break your hands.'

'There's nothing there,' I say. 'Me and Marina, just an overture. You mean – there's gangs that put their mark on her?'

'Of course,' he says, 'she's a resource. They put tattoos where you can't see. Try looking on the inside of her cheek. Wow, it must smart when first it's done!'

'I didn't think,' I say, 'or know. Lola talks of groups like ours all round and out of sight ...'

'Who cares?' says Chet. 'The gangs that's working here are what you see. The rest – well, you should know, it's all a cover-up for class ... The great campaign: philosophy, the goals, the rules – you must have read: it's all illusion stuff. Class interest, that's the solid thing—'

I interrupt, 'I didn't think we had an interest, except the talking on, and maybe sweeping out.'

'Those books that Krystal plays,' says Chet, 'they're full of stuff about the life we live, and how to manage it. It's written like it's all to come, the future all fantastic: but it's now! Those guys that throng to Krystal's tent – they read the walls, to make a sense. And afterwards, they follow up with scuttering figures, wavering words, Korky Kat, a skimming manikin – graffiti fleeting round the blocks. Some Arab guy ... started it off. It's like that Shusha, on her local show: her folks don't believe in marking with tattoos, but you can bet she's linked some way to guys who have her as resource. They don't let go.'

'I guess it's good that all belong to someone, Chet,' I say. 'The guys I worked with in the terror biz – when they gave up, and when the lake went dry – they made a porno band. Boy! how they pranced. Team spirit – that was what they had.'

'Of course,' says Chet, 'we all heard of the group – the Spy Boys, ex The Flames. There's lots of money there, much more than in some politics, and chasing guys and caging them ...'

'I found it tough,' I go on, 'not to belong at all. Some god, some gang, a corporation or a country – or a band – you need some guys to play along with you.'

'A band's the best,' says Chet, quite wisely. 'First, it was hunters and the dance, now it's just the dance. The music – it plays everywhere, all day and night.'

'Sure,' I say. 'To Krystal I belonged. To Lola now,' and Chet says, 'Calm down, young Jan. No one belongs to anyone for long. Better be a trumpeter, and set the time.'

We stare, we turn away. Neither of us can play anything.

I say, 'Class struggle and ballet. Yes, most of the super guys have tried that, or something like – the message interclass, and then arm wrestling, playing the sax, they've tried it all. You should write a book, Chet, give that idea some space.'

'Oh, I have. You bet I have. But if anything was up to books ...' he says.

I say, 'Maybe we should take music lessons. It is the only way. It's much too late for communism, self-control is démodé. My girlfriend's boyfriend, long ago, he played the clarinet. It was salvation, till they burnt his instrument ...'

Chet nods and nods: 'There's the pure truth,' he says. 'Though parts of how you put the tale – they seem a touch

153

pathetic. But maybe it's too late for lessons now. Things move so fast, they'll leave us far behind.'

'Or, we could ask to join the Roof, have Krystal make more cash, and we'd be rich, not have to skim it off ...'

Chet says, 'Still riches? That's the game, for you? Too late, too late.'

'No, Chet. I'll just serve my time. That's it. Maybe Marina...'

When I look at him, my friend, good Chet – there's something, when you've once been in Intelligence – it's like the song says, about the finger of suspicion, points at you, at everyone ..

'Chet,' I ask. 'You and Marina screw?'

'Oh no,' he says, 'and that was long ago.'

I ask Marina, when we are alone, 'you and Chet, then – you weren't caught? Those guys that marked you as resource, they didn't guess?'

'No,' she says.

'Then – just a curiosity – inside your mouth, a thing I'd like to check ...'

'Fuck off,' she says.

And in the end, so what. The kicking, though, Chet's right. Avoid it if I can.

'Those were the years,' says Lola, 'when we had some cash, and we'd Intelligence to keep us safe.'

They say if you're resettled, you go down the mines. They're digging out the earth, the underground, the underneath, the inner core, the last resource. That's another thing – avoid it, digging, if you can.

'Ah China,' Lola says, and laughs. 'But don't go down their mines!'

'This is the good life,' Marina says. 'You needn't bed with anyone, like them or not, or talk of love, or battles past. The trouble is, there's always someone waiting, who'll walk in and break it all.'

'Nonsense,' Lola says, 'We have a structure, strong and tangible. It will prevail. A lot of it is me.'

That's the trouble, lots of it.

'Who's to come, and steal our nothing?' asks Lola, of us, her faithful band. 'Our talks, our teasing through eternal truths – that is our sword, our spade. Our *spada*. Cheaper than smack, reversible too.'

'Krystal may come, unless we join her first,' says Chet.

I notice Lola's grubbier than the rest of us. The sari has no end to tuck, it's drabbled on the floor, and frayed, the couch where she reclines is rather stained. And yet – she keeps her weight up, like a wrestler, pinning guys down with argument. Brava, Lola! In for the kill!

'Those look like cops,' says Chet. 'They're coming up the drive. They must have left their carriages outside. They're marching on our castle here ...'

We laugh. Yes they are cops, they're large, they move like toads, the colour's right, the gait as well, if toads walked upright. Lola says, 'They look like Russian cops.' Indeed they do. There is a chant, we hear 'Tatarva...'

'How very interesting!' Lola says. 'Perhaps they think we're Tatars – as you know,' she turns to me, convinced I don't. 'It's right and logical. Every group that lives round here, they have their cops, and local cares ...' and on she goes. 'Now, Tatar history ...'

To me, it's clear that Krystal's found a group of cops.....

'Run!' says Chet. 'There is no stigma! There's no shame!' And off we go.

'Split!' shouts Chet. 'Uptown you, and me downtown ...' We don't know which is which – here it's all flat. We split – the buildings here are fine, up to the second floor at least, the bricks with liver-colours – the purple-brown with staring lizard eyes of white, the fatal pustules, tiny flaws, the fat, the vodka clawmarks, others bright orange, crimson lake, or postbox red, like children's watercolour paints.

I find a subway, down – oh no, a flight of stairs, and then it's blocked, there's sound of guys beneath, they dig. I fall ten steps, then turn and climb and as I run, I pass a toad-cop, coming down. He doesn't recognise, he thinks it's someone rising from below, on down he goes.

You need to eat to run and breathe, my lungs are flat and acid. I just stand and hurt.

Here's the graffiti, going round... – and then the memory comes to me: – the toad-cops, in a strip Salm showed me. No uniforms, but wearing their grey-yellow skin, original. I press against the wall, the figures run across me, going fast, they turn the corner, and at once they're coming back around the block – some story, of encounters, bad love, a touch of torment, here's a woman's face, you almost feel the pain, but no – it slides on past, there goes some sex, and now she's running too, how quick it goes, no one can follow this – the black sketched out on brick, and now, it shows a spacious town, it's being shelled, and now there's tears and someone close to her ... she scoots on past, and round the corner. Running, running – they take her in, some guys – oh no! it's torturers again, and she breaks free, and round and round the block she goes, and then I see across the street – the story is the same, graffiti on the opposite block, same story,

156

quick as quick. I press myself against the wall. Maybe I'll be invisible, the story passing over me, much quicker than I run.

The woman, and the chase, they skim around me, over me. I think of Nikki. An encounter. Skimming over – clouds that run across the sun.

I like real toads – stubborn, solemn, climbing everywhere on tiny hills. They see the joke.

It's quiet – no one runs after, and today, the hunt is done.

I go back to Lola's place: 'Chet! Where did you go?' I ask. Lola broods, she seems not to have moved from where she languishes.

'A bar. I'm used to not being somewhere,' Chet says, 'but Lola. They did her over.'

Well, there she is. Not a kicking, though. A bad message.

She says, 'I got me a hit in the eye. My eye. An accident? What do you reckon, Jan? Marina – she knew exactly what she wanted, where to go. There's water, oceans, all around here. She went to one of those to hide.'

'You don't seem bothered, Lola,' says Chet, affectionately.

'Well,' she says, 'I say this. Those weren't Russian cops. They were guys dressed as Russian cops.' We laugh.

'Now,' says Lola, 'something has changed. We should change with it,' and she says how this place was immense, and even if there's only one in a thousand that's still here, survived, above ground, that still leaves thousands, more than you could meet, or recognise – if you even wanted to.

'Candide!' she says. 'If you travel, that's the only way to be. Think of the Mexicans, all of them. And Rio! Never, ever, would you meet them all, or even get to know one, really well; or choose at random, even know one superficially. Life: that shows it's not a fiction, not where the characters are limited in number, or all flagged up – "this one's a president, a general, a father, or a whore".'

'What did Krystal want?' asks Chet.

'More peace,' says Lola. 'For her, not me.'

The 'Next Move' goes on 'The Roof'

'To Krystal's brawn we'll add me,' Lola says. 'As I am. Beef.' It's true. She can't move off the palanquin.

'You bastards,' she says to me and Chet, 'You peripatetics! Just ran off, and left.'

'It's their nature,' says Marina, sidling in with seaweed draped around.

'How's your eye, Lola?' Chet asks. It's her excuse to be carried down to Krystal's tent.

'I see fewer things, but further into them,' she says, suffering.

'Beware,' says Marina, 'Seers get burnt – in a tar barrel on the beach. People dancing round.'

'Well,' says Lola. 'It's good to see them dance. At least the culture's left them that.'

It's a rare sight: we needed elephants, and trumpeters, of course, and nimble dwarves. A parade. We strain to lift the sofa with her on. In Lola there's no wind at all. Just substance – 'Essence,' she corrects. What weight, signifying nothing.

'Use the carrying poles,' shouts Lola. So we do.

Here's Krystal, all in wool. Alan, sour. Shusha on a screen. No Nikki. Krystal says,

'The middling guys elsewhere – they prosper, dine on wallabies in ginger sauce. But we – are still cut off ...'

'And stride – to our extinction,' Lola says. 'At least we'll write the history of our tribe. Those courtship rituals – hedgehog on hedgehog, Jan, Marina, Chet ... My wisdom ... inscribed on golden plates ...'

'I hear it now,' says Alan, '"This is the final, decisive battle..." I'll put it as a waltz, maybe a trot. With Lola, you can't do a march.'

'Well now,' Lola says, not pleased. 'Who's this?'

A skinny lad's come in.

'A painless birth!' says Krystal. 'Karl from Nagpur, so he says. Just walked in off the street. Feeds himself, and dresses. Sings to us. Writes songs, pours drinks. Right now he's buying debt. We've more than anyone. He says it's worth. One day, they'll pay it off ...'

'The silly boy,' says Alan, sourer still.

'Nagpur,' asks Marina. 'That's not by the sea?'

'No, no, that's somewhere else,' says Karl. 'By ship, you'd get quite close, I guess.'

'Those movies!' says Marina. 'The life, the beat, all tick-tock neat. The sea! The colours ...'

'Yes,' says Karl, 'the sea is pink, and white, and black – and cadmium.'

'I know, I know,' Marina says. 'I imagine it, just so.'

She thinks awhile. 'And is it true,' she asks. 'That when you guys all die, you turn back into monkeys – quite religious ones?'

'Well,' says Karl. 'Not everyone believes ...'

'And is it true,' Marina asks. 'Not everybody has to die?'

Karl says, 'All that you've heard is partly true,' and she is satisfied, and Karl as well.

'This debt,' asks Lola. 'Is it quite secure? It sounds a bit like smoke.'

'No, no,' says Krystal. 'Karl is right. And if he's not, we've hired some guys who'll get the money back for us. If guys eventually can't pay, then we'll forgive them, under the Roof they'll go, contrite. And loyal. And, Lola, that's where you come in afterwards – the "Next Move". Where all is golden light.'

'Yes, that I see,' says Lola, primping up. 'But guys like Jan – and Alan. They don't have a role.'

'Jan is intelligence,' says Krystal. 'He calculates the risk. And Alan – well, this boy Karl, he organises the parades, he sings the songs. Alan's a difficulty ...' and the ladies parley on.

'No, absolutely not!' I say. 'I've been and done Intelligence. I'm smarter now. No more in Julie's dreams, and falling off the ship, and alpine meadows, cornflowers blue as eyes, anenomes in tantric colours ... no, you two, that's hokum. I love hokum, obviously, but not to make it a career ...'

'You're crazy, Jan,' says Lola brisk and pure, and Krystal says she'll have me back, contrite and loyal, but doing what serves best.

'And that leaves Alan,' Lola says. 'Marina is our link with gangs – but Alan, fusty religion, adolescent doubts, what's to become of him?'

'You guys don't understand,' says Alan, feeling for his neck. 'All this tradition stuff from Karl – it all seems new because you're ignorant – the juice belongs to someone else, and you're attracted by the husks ...'

There's a sound from the wrestling mat in the corner. 'Look!' says Lola, 'Karl and Marina, playing.'

'That's not play,' says Alan, crossly, 'that is something else. Called "taking us to India".'

So it seems.

'Karl just thinks of being rich, and setting up this business,' Alan says. 'And that's the old way. It won't work – besides, this is my country, and if anyone is rich, it should be me.'

Chet's gone, walked out. True to himself. His namesake.

My life – so far has been adventure. But – does it add up to something, tell something more ...? What I should do. Next – that's a good word. What should I do next?

'Karl tells wonderful stories,' Lola says. 'He's quite entranced Marina. Shusha was never up to anything like that ...'

'Where could Karl take us, then?' I ask. 'Justice in Central Asia – I had enough of that ...'

'The justice was perfect,' Krystal says. 'A crime there was – the trees, the people. And you got off.'

Alan reminds us – 'Salm says we're at our end. Him running his graffiti everywhere. His guys are fighting for their lives, but ours – they turned the future into cash, he said – a dream that didn't work. People work, he said, not dreams.' Alan paces about. He's at his end. He needs the work ... and Lola says,

'This Alan guy – how can he be reactionary, without a past?'

'Me – a rigorous fogey!' Alan says. 'It's just another trick, a new one, possibly. Maybe those goddam trees, those people, were more important ... I know nothing about trees. It seems there's something more you need ... Besides, those apples aren't for wisdom, they are for repentance, guilt, all that stuff. They say that in the end, the basket's going down with all of us inside, together to the end, snapping and biting, like a knot of scorpions. Not that I object – being one myself, a scorpion, I quite appreciate ...'

'So, Alan,' Krystal says. 'It's maybe you're the one that's left behind.' And I remember Julie saying maybe no one gets abandoned – but if we're in the basket, all of us, and going down, being thrown overboard is nothing special ... and with that, I comfort Alan.

'If I don't fit with you – you fit with me,' says Alan. 'I love you, every one.'

'How pathetic,' Krystal says. 'He never mucked in.'

'We were a caravan,' says Alan, tearfully. 'Not like societies – full of cyphers. The rich guys who killed people and tarnished riches. The poor guys who got killed, didn't care, and sat in their chair. We were a different band.'

'Yes,' says Krystal. 'We toured the world and vodka was our incense.'

'Alan,' says Karl. 'If you must leave, try to live in purity. If you can stay, bear heavier loads.'

'Fuck off, Karl,' shouts Alan. 'Hit-men and whores – that's where these heavy loads originate!'

'Go, Alan, fight!' shouts Lola. 'Resist, resist!'

'I want to write country songs for clean people,' Alan pleads. We're all crying now, more or less, it's like *La Bohème* – the dreadful end is overwhelming. We treat him bad, he loves us – goodbye, Alan, we loved you too, though not so much.

'Don't be a crybaby, Alan,' Krystal says. 'An up is followed by a down – that's physics. Think of Ziad, gone where no one cries. And Shusha too – gone to defend her civilisation, forward or back, who knows. How they fight dirty, those guys! Maybe it's all worth it – back to the roots, or forward to the flowers. I'm not a judge! Her shows are all on tape, they last eternity. My, what a following she has! Then off she went – her last, her decisive battle. Someone wins, no doubt ...'

She doesn't say, 'And then?'

We're faced with Alan's tears, and so we seek a middle way, some hybrid state – you take the pain, but smiles are on their way.

'Poor Shusha,' Lola says, not knowing her. 'Another one who's disappeared. What neighbours! I hope she knows how it turns out – isolation, or be like the rest? Best to be in this hole, forgotten and unsought ...'

'No, no,' shouts Karl, 'I'll raise you up.' We stare at him. Our hearts are full of hope, we'll not admit defeat.

'Onward,' shouts Krystal in reply. 'No mountains, though, no animals, no sudden deaths.'

'I can't wait to get on board that ship!' Marina says. 'Like Ulysses. Out of this dump.'

'You'll need to walk a bit as well,' says Karl, and winks at me. 'Nagpur's not on the beach.'

'They talk of ships that sail,' says Alan. 'But for centuries, there's only been a churn and throb they make.'

'Alan, I protected you,' says Krystal. 'In my way. But now the sharks are hungry ...'

On the wall, the screen, there's Shusha: 'civilisation, shops, this way; that way, soft freedoms in the house, the cult, hard duties too,' and Krystal says, 'Poor Shusha – arguing the case will make her vulnerable. Then she'll disappear,' and Lola says that when there's guys with guns who're after you, there is no middle way, 'That's where her lifestyle, her philosophy – it lets you down, though it's derived from mine,' and Karl's impatient, tells Marina,

'In India, the poor are happy, underneath – the bad time implies the better, it's in the language we all learned.'

'I don't need believe you, Karl,' Marina says, 'but still it's wonderful, to hear you talk like that.'

'That load of debt,' says Alan. 'Mind it doesn't sink your boat.'

'It's wealth,' says Karl. 'And taken care of,' and he winks at me again.

'No, I'm not complicit,' I say, 'of no one, not for anything.'

Lola says, 'The boy Karl – he's such a dear. A lovely colour, too. Now Plato says the colours go together, naturally ... harmony is harmony, better than melody, for sure. Or was it Aristotle?'

We don't know.

Finally, Krystal shouts, 'OK, OK. We'll take the ship. Maybe I can start a circus there, in India, wherever we drop off – I bet the Russians haven't come. The right colour ... yes – that's the clinch. It's true in India there's trees and fighting everywhere – but no doubt room for us as well,' and Lola says, for sure, there's elephants to take her weight, guys there do philosophy all through the night – Marina's jumping with delight ... my job, to guard the two old awful women.

Alan left behind.

The Ship

'Is that the ship? Of course it is,' Marina says.

There's Alan on the shore. He's brought a kitbag. It says 'Private' on it. I never knew he fought some war. He'll not come with us. There's his band – is that a Kaddish? Or a Requiem?

It's maybe all the same – in any case, inaudible up here. The choir – their mouths pop open, shut, like fish mouths in a dough. He gestures, as we move away – there's the umbrella sign; that one is Greek – two hands, a flap of some great augured bird. Alan, goodbye – guilty of nothing, save for being Alan, his life sentence – and I think of all the others, disappeared, as he folds his baton, cases it, and turns and ... disappears. The only one who isn't with us and who hasn't disappeared – is Nikki. No sax in the band, as Alan says, the sax is what you play in corners at a party, to be alone, and ruminate.

Chet. Maybe he's among the crew. He said coincidence is sometimes all that you can get. Perhaps he lays coincidences, like elephant traps, along the forest floor, engineering them. In you fall – there he is to pick you out. Here's a sailor – could be Chet, his shirt says 'Gift of ...' rather frayed.

'Hi!' I say. He turns, a coppery face – it isn't Chet. There's a coincidence ...

'You know,' the sailor says, 'the pressure down there in the depths – it seems to me a black hole fell down there, for that is where they finish up. The moon has oceans too, you know, and then there's Mars, and planets you can't see all round. And bits of black have surely flaked, and down they go, and maybe there are fish that live in darkest depths – you drop a light, it seems it is the sun, and up they rise, explode. That's what they call a denizen. Black holes.'

I must get rid of him: I say, 'We've taken ship to go to India. Nagpur.'

'It seems to me,' he says, quite kind and slow, 'we don't stop there no more.'

I wish he had been Chet: that voice – 'how could you know what love is?' he sang, and now maybe we'll never know. We're leaving, we see the shore recede, it's like Dufy, the beach is tutti-frutti ice, yumyum, but those are dogs and towels, those coloured whisps – a breeze that always blows as if to raise the flag of partyland ... neat breasts in tiny pouches – it is France, like many many years ago. The pier ... too bad, there'll come the storm and sweep it out to sea and total loss. And no one knows it yet.

The sailor says, 'You know, we don't take food on board. You have to fish, and if there's none you catch, it's like a shipwreck in reverse. The ship sails on, the sea is flat, your comrades are too tough to eat ... you shout to passing ships – "fish, fish! throw us some fish" – they laugh and on they sail.'

Imagine – going down, the spratlings, little silver sprites, does each one need an image of itself? All that sea, mirror profound – you think of looking glass, but each *alice*, little anchovy, it never sees itself ... and then the herrings, hake, and haddocks – see their eyes! – in layers, all alliterate, like a game – and spidery things, those creepy feelers, spokes without meat – my, they're expensive ... now there's nothing, dark – yes, the matelot is right, this is where black holes end up and start, the pressure, like a universal box: lead suit.

The cities that we pass ... the battlements are different cakes, the blue umbrellas! aloes – big green gastropods, right at the water's edge. Let's go ashore! – oh no, how sad to see the habitations fade away, can't stop, won't stop. If only Nikki ... all excitement, because you didn't know a thing about her, and she hadn't time for you. Another folly, another voyage not quite undertaken – as the song says, '*Je n'ai jamais vu la Chine, mais je l'imagine.*' Another song, wisdom-packed like all of them.

'We'll all have to work so hard, but I don't mind.' It's Marina. We're still all tied up to the dock. She says, 'We'll see nowhere till we're in India. Think of it – the monkeys, snakes, elephants. All those people, the same lovely colour!'

'Marina,' I say. 'I have a special feeling for you ...' and she interrupts, 'Yes, yes, me too. I always thought if things were different ... about me, how I feel.'

'Yes,' I say, 'things would be different.' I think of Nikki. Marina says,

'But Karl's all movement. The new.'

'Look, Marina,' I say, 'there is a scam, must be. That debt, it's worth what you can force the guys ...'

'Yes, yes,' she says, 'I know! It's fun!'

'There must be more,' I say.

'He reads to me,' she says, 'no one did that before to me. A little book – some guy called Rameau. His nephew.'

'Yes, we did it all at school,' I say. 'That was the best.' She starts to tell the plot – neither remembers it too well.

We settle Lola, her divan, on deck. 'The captain says it gets quite brisk up here,' she says. 'I want to see Greek cities, battlements like different cake,' in hope, she stares out through the waves. 'The trouble is,' she says, 'these jobless whiteys on the shore,' indeed, there's lots, 'They wouldn't make good slaves. In India, there's all the hands you need. The Greeks have learnt to do their cleaning by themselves.'

'We'll go past Spain,' says Karl. 'The kings there used artillery to hunt the game. Those were the days! Abundance ...'

'Then there's Italy, the pirates ...!' says Marina, 'and forest nymphs. What do they eat, I wonder? Some immortals roam as stags and such, others are bushes – life is complex there – you have to watch your lunch.'

I ask, 'Karl, Marina, how'd you know so much?'

'We did it all at school,' they say.

'Come, come,' says Krystal. 'Chet'll materialise for sure, and not as bush or stag, or golden rain. Talking of which, since Alan's dumped for disbelieving everything in general, and we believe in almost everything, you'll join me now, you guys, in an auspicious song.'

With reservations, we link arms and sing, 'Lead golden light, amidst th'encircling gloom', and at the end, Krystal says, 'Go to, go to, for Karl has signed you on as crew. A thrifty move. So, Jan – off you go, behind the bar. Karl – watch for mermaids from the top, Marina – flying fishes for our tea ...'

All this we set ourselves to do. We haven't moved. Chet doesn't show. Nor anyone.

I'm shaking up the cocktails – Liferafts, Leeward shoals – my specialities, and 'Gie's a toot,' the sailor pleads. The captain joins us, drinks – tequila, finest sea salt, 'limes for the scurvy'. We're all living high: I say, 'Should we not untie the boat and leave?'

'No, no,' the captain shouts, 'we come back here whenever we have sailed the sea. So, let us cut things short, stay put. Besides, a single matelot will not suffice to stoke the fires, to point the ship and make landfalls, and watch for wrecks and wrack, and inauspicious birds.'

'The captain's drunk,' the sailor says, 'so we should try to join him, sacrificing for fair winds. When we set off, we need to keep this bit of land behind us. And then, in time, it all turns round – and there is land before.'

'No, no, you fools,' shouts Karl. 'The guys we're waiting for ...' It could be Chet. Or Nikki. But it's not. It's smugglers. Smugglers. 'Every good trip needs smugglers,' Krystal says. 'It's known as free trade, among the good guys.' We tie Lola and her sofa to the deck. We're under way, it's brisk, just like the captain said, and water comes on board. 'It's all for good guys, the stuff below,' the chief smuggler says – Tonino, we can call him. Karl insists,

'The smuggler guys – they helped to sell the debt – the guys that owed us found refusing hard, there were so many of us. They paid up something, then we bought this stuff. It's parcels, we shall drop them off along the way. Some of them's on wheels.'

'And shall we get to Nagpur?' asks Marina.

'Well,' says Karl, 'everyone's from somewhere. I'm from Nagpur, though it doesn't mean you're always going back to where you start.'

'Of course we shall,' says Krystal. 'Laws of physics – that's another one. You never really leave, when once you start. It's in your bones, like seaside rock,' and then she says, 'One trouble is – the captain steers a wobbly course – he should have stuck to vodka,' and it's true, those engines somewhere, bellydeep, are labouring; those goddam inauspicious birds throng round us, and we've not yet left the dock.

'When we arrive some place,' says Karl, 'Marina can drive Ferraris off. Me and the lads, we'll take those heavy macho boxes, and consign.'

We've left at last. Some Greek was into cosmic mathematics, and he's left Lola with a counting of the waves. 'It's all a plan, design,' she says. 'You count and count, the numbers click on in the sky, and circle round, and keep us safe...' and on she goes. The matelot's not sure – he's further into space than she.

I work all day and night: we are a happy ship, some smugglers pray and some pass out, a hold is full of vodka, and when I've time I paint the ship from end to end, till Krystal shouts – 'Risk, Jan, risk! That is your job,' and so I tell her risk's incalculable, and she's satisfied. 'Well, Jan,' she says, 'I need an expert in it, that is all.'

The sea! The sea! If you are desperate, I understand you like to see it, if there's ferries taking you back home. But otherwise it's grey, and grey above, or blue, and much the same. Its pointless restlessness, its moods from pitch to roll, its jumping up to bathe you, its sucking wallows, sweepings, junk... Is this my old frigate? Refloating, portless round and round the world, those horn fanfares that summon the valkyries – those goddam black birds, the white ones too, wide as bombing drones...

I hear from Lola, 'Fuck off, birds! I curse you, in the names of Democritus, Epicurus – either the world is sticky, or it's crumbs. So what. You birds – bringers of pestilence, eaters of our dead .... I call on Lord Megistus – get you gone ...' She sprawls, magnificent, the sari silver ... no, it's salt and crap from albatross ...

Karl says, 'It's dreams we trade – arms for freedom, dope for happiness – these automobiles – my, how fast you speed! Tarmac beneath, cement on either side ... better to find an elephant, your friend for life, and there, you're looking down on everyone.'

Lola does philosophy, of course, 'That's why guys cruise. To see the sea, which doesn't give a clue to human aims, just rolls and dips. Ask the unanswerable – that's the teacher's trick,' and so she does. The smugglers rouse, they chant and sing, 'It's empirio-criticism that we learn today.' The captain too, he reads his text – and then he says:

'My friends, that lesson gets the problematic right: – I think I may have missed that tiny hole, the orifice, umbilical, that takes us from the sea into another sea.'

'You've missed the Greeks!' shouts Lola. 'You tosspot!'

Marina too is in distress: 'The flying fish are grounded here – I wave my nets – there's zero food.'

'Vodka all round,' says Krystal, brisk and clean. 'You seek that tiny hole – the monkey rock, and then there's more of Spain ... I'm sure you did it all at school. The Med – that's where Medes lived, not the Persians, though,' and on she goes to show her classic bent: 'It's thick thread through the needle's eye, to sail from ocean into sea. The simile's the way: you close your eye, and then the thread slips through the needle's slit, as if it's charmed.'

And that we try, we lie around on deck, and close our eyes.

It works. We're past the monkeys, here is more of Spain, and other countries too, all round, just like they were in school.

A braided officer climbs up the side. 'Oh no,' says Karl, 'We have no dope, no arms. That's government trade. Some classic cars, is all.'

We take him to the vodka hold, he drinks, and then Karl says, 'Maybe I have the automobile that makes the cultural link from us to you. We who sail romantic seas remember smugglers, pirates, battles gentlemanly – an old-style fighting, muskets and cannons, all that stuff. I can propose, in friendship' – he unwraps a crate '– here's a Cutlass, vintage, lizard green ...' The officer's impressed. They parley. We sail on. The officer stays on board, he starts the Cutlass engine, toots the horn. The smugglers shout, 'Cutlasses for everyone,' and Krystal says the customs guys who pry into the contraband are weak and greedy human stuff.

'Here, we're all good guys,' Karl says, cuddling the officer: 'Trade drives the world, it makes the peace, and art. And labour too, meeting new guys, and also leaving where you're at, and setting sail ...'

'All true, how true,' the braided searcher says. 'How do I get my Cutlass off your boat?'

'Enough, enough!' shouts Krystal. 'All this drink, and hermeutics too – it's all too much...Some journeys – to the moon, or to world's end, the end of night, of time, to China, Ithaca – illuminate. Ours is crumbling into tat: Italian pirates – kitsch. Greece a desert. Salm and Shusha – where they ought to be, they've disappeared, a-skittering round the walls, it seems. Chet didn't show – he's lots of kids, he makes a tour, and when he's bored, he sires some more. There's lots of his in Italy, we should have found him there. But – we've accomplished nothing – drink, and talk, and goddam birds, and weather too terrible to describe.'

'Yes, Krystal, that's all so,' Marina says, 'but – those stuffed aubergines in Izmir – never to forget!'

'We haven't got to Turkey yet,' says Krystal, 'and save the discourse on the food. My throat is papered thick with fins. If I could do without my meals, I would.'

She stumps along the deck.

All round there's bits of boat with guys – hundreds, all looking inward, not at the waves, staring at another bunch of guys, hunched, staring back. It's like the history again, of guys from Africa who crossed the sea, the land bridge, civilisation in their heads, and bringing it to whiteys in the north ... Then, Krystal turns to us and shouts – 'You bastards! Greed! Self-gratification. Bourgeois without a bourgeoisie, disowned. Chancers, wide boys and spivs. That's you, you semi-criminals.

You parasites without a host – you suck each other dry, and lick the husks ... You scrabblers!'

'Calm yourself,' Marina says. 'You can't mean to pick those poor guys up, that's drifting here, when we are journeying – the golden light, remember that!'

'Krystal, my dear,' says Karl, 'you surely wouldn't want that we abandon you on shore, and let you fight alongside some guys ...'

'No, no, you fools,' shouts Krystal, 'I'm not mad, though you would have me so! I'd put these guys to work for me, of course. The problem isn't them – it's you! Dung-beetles, every one.'

We call the captain – he is down below, he has a suite of rooms with chandeliers. He is no help.

'Call Lola, she alone can mollify our Krystal. It's the waves,' I say. 'The repetition. Brings to mind a life of toil, then tumbling in her grave, worn through. It's called the madness of the sea – a heaving discontent ...' I'd tell them of the apple forest, and the animals who ran away, all that, but they have gone to stir up Lola. I hear her – she complains, 'Not now, I've lessons to prepare. About those guys, philosophers, that don't quite grasp the meaning of a word – quite fascinating, but a little dull. I hope the smugglers understand – they're used to speak in gesture, touching the face – that must mean more to them than orders given by some guy who shouts. "The gestural oblique" – that is my theme ...' She would go on, but now, her task's to pacify. She rises. In the vertical, she's more impressive still. It's the first time she's troubled to stand up.

'Krystal, you goddam nuisance,' she exclaims. 'Sort out your problem. You're from some underworld, so concentrate on being that, a harridan, and nothing more.'

Krystal seems quite calm, but then she screams, 'If I'd my tits, I'd cut one off, and show you how to lead a band of lady warriors! Just drop me off ...' and the officer revs up his Cutlass, ready to be landed.

Krystal shouts, 'The left, the left, I'll fight for rights ...' and on she raves ...

I say, 'Krystal, we all agree, but maybe this is not the place...' There's sand, a track, but lady warriors not in sight: 'You'll end up disappeared, like Ziad, or like Salm. And Shusha,' and I shed some tears, to think of all who've not been seen for months, or only as cartoons, and Nikki, not disappeared, but just not there, and all the others named or not, who're being grafted, spliced, or stood in pots, awaiting some rebirth or new acquaintanceship, or Julie's 'maybe I love you' – some crap remark like that which starts a Trojan war ... and then I say,

'If only Chet were here ...' and Krystal says,

'Love of my life. Dear Chet. Just see him once, and follow him, you love him, can't wait to bear his child – he is the golden light ... "How could you know what love is ...?" Show me, show me, Chet. Is all I ask.'

It's terrible, her weakness – here, there's bosses all around, and if your boss is craven, there's no hope. This was the risk, incalculable..and now it's here. I've dedicated all my life to kneeling down before some cheese, big, small, ripe or musty – that's what Intelligence was for, to find a boss who didn't let you down, and kept you fed, and told you you were free, and sexy too, if that was apposite.

'Look!' says Marina, to distract. 'Look! There's pyramids and sphinxes. How wonderful.'

'What's wonderful?' asks Krystal angrily. 'They were there yesterday, probably tomorrow. Some things go like that – not many, but what's the big surprise? Time has its dull routine. What you want – revolution in jumps? Stuff on the ground – it's fixed.' She turns to Maria, 'Unless your boyfriend's trying to root them up? The little spiv; wide boy; petty dip.'

'Oh yes,' Marina says, quite eagerly. 'That's why he's special. If he was a big boss – that would be awful. Suits, bad breath, all that.'

The matelot puts in – 'You guys – here we should hang a right. That's the way to India, otherwise you'll walk a long long way.'

'No,' Lola says, 'Krystal is right. This Karl's a vagabond – and now he's got the cash, the smugglers all went home to dandle kids, a lesson's maybe on the way for him.'

They stand over Karl, and threaten. My, Lola's big, erect, a grizzly. All those teeth ...

Marina will protect Karl, maybe – but, we're all divided, with no time to think and take a side. If Chet were here ... Instead, the captain says, 'Back off. No fighting on my boat. First principle, no swords or cutlasses: we drop this good guy off, his Cutlass too.' And so he does. The guy, expert in all sorts of customs, gets set to drive his motor off. Tonino, other smugglers, and the matelot – they race away upon the sand – some give umbrella signs as well.

'Now,' says the captain, 'watch the sign.'

It's flashing: 'End of trip.'

'At last!' says Krystal, 'and at least. We're somewhere. No more water for me for a while. It's deserts from now on.'

I think, is this my destiny – with Lola, journeying through the waves, to take philosophy to India? Marina, cuddled up with Karl? And pouring drinks while Krystal shouts and sneers? And ending up so far from Nikki, all the rest?

On ships, there's always heavy metal stuff, just lies around – it may be anchors, or for use on pirates, terrorists – this is a tiny world, you need to be prepared for sudden storms and sinkings. Krystal says to me, 'You hold that silly girl, Marina, we will do the rest,' and Lola says, 'The greater good – that line, it always wins. You pose it as dilemma, but you knock his head, his *head*,' she shouts to Krystal. 'But in the end there's always circumstance that shows you win the moral case. Those arms, the dope Karl brought – it's true, it all went off to good guys, that's for sure, and that was why we didn't balk – but how are we to know? It's all intentions, and their consequences ...' on she goes, philosophy is friend at last.

They hit him – Karl expires.

Marina says,

'No, no, don't leave me, stuck with Jan. I wanted Karl, and though he's met his end – this Jan's too weird, a creepy type ...' and then she weeps. I hold her tight, while Karl is finished off. The money's safe, the ladies count, maybe they will divide...

'Oh well,' the captain says, 'I tried non-violent arguments, but now the deed is done, and we should take some good from Karl, and so the moral balance tilts to parity,' and Lola says, that is a principle of fairness, justice emerging from an unjust world, or circumstance. And so the captain shouts, and tells the customs guy, 'Come back – we have some organs for you.'

There they are: the organs. In death, Karl's pieces offer hope and life to countless more. They lie like bits of pulp and pips, but surely they will serve for some sad guy who's lost his own.

'Good comes from bad,' says Lola. 'That is true in India, and China too, no doubt, if they have got that far.'

'Indians know all about philosophy, Lola,' says Marina. 'Except the dull bits. And – I'm really sad my lover's been dispersed, though good will come of where he's spread.'

I say, 'Marina, maybe we should leave the ship. These epic voyages repeat. Remember, there's the magician and the pigs, the one-eyed macho guy – that's all to come. We're innocent, we didn't kill, we could leave the ship and go ...'

'Innocent?' Marina says. 'You held me back.'

'To keep you safe, my dear,' I say. 'It's always been my job. That is intelligence – the tree inclines before the storm. Especially the apple tree. Or else. It splits.'

'Well,' she says, reluctantly, 'the captain's here, and he could marry us. That way your fortune's halfway mine. And legally we're complicit.'

'No, no,' I say. 'No fortune's come to me; besides, the captain's tight. No marriage, then. Marina – it's right you are unhappy – then, after, you will happy be. It's another Krystal law of physics. Just relax.'

'You sound so long ago,' Marina says.

Down the plank, we're on the shore; there's almost a corniche. 'You haven't thought it through,' she says: 'What we do here. The people back there, on the ship, Lola, Krystal – what becomes of them, of us?'

'It's not the people bothers me,' I tell her. 'It's the casing, the habitat, what you're bound to do. It's Krystal's laws of physics – the contexts pull more than gravity.'

That sailor had it right – there's black holes, sucking energy, all round.

Sfax – good name. I wonder if it's here? I'd always hoped to go ...

'Look!' Marina shouts. 'Elephants and monkeys! We're in India after all.'

'No, no,' I say. 'It's just cartoons. They run them round the walls. It must be all the rage. What's left of revolutionary cinema. Just movement now.'

Marina says, 'It's strange, but you and I, we don't seem to meet good guys. You say you gave your life for them.'

I don't contradict. She goes on, 'Karl wasn't a good guy, I guess.'

'No,' I say, 'but he was vigorous. That's maybe often better.'

Marina puts her face close to mine. I think she's going to kiss me. She says, 'Fuck you. You killed my love.' Chet's namesake didn't sing that, though he might. He said it with his trumpet.

We go back on board. 'Gang plank,' Marina says. 'I wonder what gang that was? It sounds perverse as well.'

'Ha!' says Krystal. 'Back for your cut, I guess.'

'I'm not giving it up,' Marina says. 'Not for anyone.'

Well, I think, what would I, shall I, do with my freedom? You strive for it, so's not to be oppressed, and then – it seems it's either power, or drudge again. Then Krystal crows,

'Now I can buy another tent. I love nomadic life!'

Marina says, 'Whatever else turns up, I'll be street trash.'

'You could be proud of that,' I say, and now she turns on me.

'You smell of death, you know, for what you've done before, and now. That is your trade, and death will come to you and taunt and leer.'

It isn't just. It's just. I think of something quite incongruous, here on our empty ship, some quote about the

178

boats, borne back ceaselessly into the past – a book, we did it all at school, the mystery of everything revealed when we were young and left us with no more to say or feel, or turn another way.

'Goodness, you're glum, you two,' says Lola, lolling back – 'I'll buy a new divan, with dwarves to fan me ... just my joke! Someone said "the rich man is the only one to whom the practice of the good comes from the soul. He" – in my case, she – "is innocent of other interests and bonds, is truly free to be example to the world – a virtuous life alone is lived when freed from worldly cares." This voyage solves some problems – others haven't yet popped up ...' and she is radiant.

'At times,' she goes on, 'I'd have thought it difficult to have a happy end, to all this pitching up and down, these fragile ships, the captain pissed and in his bunk ... the sea is full of plastic stuff, quite like a dirty kitchen sink, and mutinies, and muskets fired in sport and anger – those goddam birds, when you are lying on the deck, some perch atop and start to peck ...' She's in a trance, the rhymes come as they do, to sibyls, gurus and the like, to holy men in general. 'And all it takes is modest capital when you are done, you take your kitbag, swagger down the plank, and lurch a little with residual swell – but there you are, on land, well off, and free ...'

And Krystal says, 'The plan original is good. Not to Nagpur, for sure, but somewhere else. Maybe to look for persons disappeared, or Chet and all the rest who've not turned up. Meanwhile, to ply our trade. United in our secret, we three. Where the money came from – thanks, to Karl. Marina, the innocent, is with us too: a wise man said, the innocent by definition are most vulnerable, for, knowing what they know, their interest is in staying innocent, and keeping quiet.'

3   The Scorpions

Lara

I am a college project. Crime.

'I'm your friend. Just write me your history, all about you,' I say. The guy writes:

'... drinking with people you don't know and don't trust. No particular place to keep or gain. Off in some guy's car – "see my grannie in Silver Lake" – she's been dead for years, but we got snowed in, we drank for days. Those cars – cause lots of damage, when you drink or when you steal them. So much room up north – you can get lost for ever. Turn up for work a coupla times – they pay you off for the week to get rid ... this society, it's like a sea: you feed off the crap that sinks, it comes from guys up near the sun, wearing suits – but in their heads, the same things as yours – the game, the booze, hating the family, loving some woman, then not.

'"How much cash you got, old son?" It was a cop, I said "$6.83" – "Then," he said, "You're a vagrant, come with me," and you go in and out of jobs, and rows, and meeting up – and there's an Indian woman, keeps on coming round, I didn't know about her, maybe there's kids, a guy who has a rifle, but she's nice, we drink together, and she tells stories ...'

'I might do better with girls,' I say. 'Their criminality.'

'I don't think you give those guys their space,' Lara says. 'And from the girls you'll get harsh fun.' In the room, some brown and yellow feral cats with pointy noses – I push them gently out my way with my boot. 'There's guys, that should be interesting,' I say. 'Up at the school. An astrophysicist. Some other, into particles, or bones. It seems we started off with everything – all packed into a speck of dust.'

'We're still there,' she says.

'Hotter than hot,' I go on. 'And dense. Time zero ... can you imagine that?'

'No,' she says.

'Well, that's right,' I say. 'There's the proof. You can't. There's no place for you, to sit or stand, observe. Nothing to compare. No big or small or long or short.'

'I know,' she says. 'It's on TV.'

'Well,' I say. 'It's news to me. And they don't talk to me about it – but – I ought to know. It should be a right. Not covered up, and only certain guys who know, and they don't talk.'

'Maybe they think you're not so bright,' she says.

'They do talk about things, though, like grumbling about the food. And goddam automobiles.'

She says, 'They know you're not a prof. What was it you did – an affray? They put you into criminology, you're an exhibit. An aid. A nearly living proof. You're a crime scene. It's your sentence, it's not for learning from.' I say, 'I forgot I'm a coward. Sometimes you just join in. Sometimes you start things off. Like the universe. It's like they say in Zen – god is a dust speck on your broom.' It was me they wanted. They didn't want someone from a gang. Dead ends.

Lara insists, 'Do you tell anyone but me, you're putting a gang, a skein, together? If you find someone interesting?'

I ignore this. I say, 'And in the beginning, there were all different models, makes, of men. All black – all quite bright, religious, into painting on the walls. All competing. Stealing each others' women. So, now there's us. We're stardust, and all those African guys looped in.'

She says, 'Once Hitler was nearly as big as the world. Now he's a speck of dust on the broom, waiting to become a universe again.'

I say, 'I'm not into things so big as that. That guy – the one who broke up cars when he was drunk – he cut his woman. Cut her right up.'

'You're dark,' says Lara, 'but not quite moved outside the light. Just blocking it off.'

I say, 'Or – maybe he got scared – he thought her old man was after him. It preyed, a bit.'

'Nothing succeeds like insanity,' says Lara. 'I can't stand you, your fussy friends and their big pictures. And those punks. All you think about is making money, but you haven't got a cent. That's thought for you!'

It's all true. 'At least I don't have consciences inside my shoes, making me limp,' I say.

'I want to be free, with no one else around me,' she says. 'The college let you go. They got tired of you, so they got the cops to forget it all. That's generosity. Justice, even.'

'Well, here we are. Here we are,' I say. 'Two matches in the box.'

'You know why we're here. I saw in you – an organiser. Inspiration. Not setting up a gang for company and street nuisance, everybody saving something of themselves and passing on the crap to other people. You'd take a ride from the devil, if the bus didn't show.'

'These cats,' I say. 'You want them to recognise – this is inside. An apartment. But they've become another kind – they don't know in and out. Just food.'

'They'll learn,' says Lara, 'and if they don't, there's nothing lost.'

'They're a challenge,' I say. 'Reality's a challenge too. They say "open up to it", the tactile and the amorous, don't hide behind imagination. Be realistic, Lara. Everybody yearns for realism ...'

'You don't mean "realism",' Lara says. 'You mean "being realistic" – that's quite other.'

'Well,' I say, 'the astroman – he'll never travel to those stars, or lie back on some beach and have them tan his little legs. And bones – those black guys tucked away inside the moderns: the other prof, guy – he doesn't see them, throwing spears and joshing. Just callipers and skulls.'

She doesn't answer. There has been no question. For the moment, we are here, exasperated.

A gang. Alcohol. It's all dangerous.

'You have to learn the dangers, so's to live with them quite easily. Look at Alma, now,' says Lara. 'She lost all her family ... and the family before that too, all in one swoop.'

'It doesn't back you up,' I say. 'You foresee danger, but it's unforeseeable. As Alma found, those peoples and their states – they were quite murderous. Once they get railways and the telegraph, there's no escape. What can you say? Fine poems on the tombs, and plan your getaway?'

'You feel lost, in your loss,' says Lara. 'Though it's not particularly yours. Loss belongs to everyone. But – you should watch to see who comes out with a smile.'

'Lara,' I say, 'do you still arrange things? It seems pathetic, you know.'

'We don't have many things, my dear,' she says. 'Your friends, the gang you'd like to have – they don't count for much. The idea's worth more than the individuals,' and she goes on.

'OK,' I say. 'It was a bad idea. A flying wedge, red nail. Assertion, testing the limits – hitting guys. It wouldn't prove ... besides, what is it that needs a proof? Here we all are. Some cannibals, some just seasick, all looking for another boat.'

It's not the furniture we haven't got that Lara puts in order. Not pictures on the walls, or words in songs she doesn't sing. Arranging. She can arrange just about anything that comes to mind, and you can't see unless she tells.

'I think a lot when you're not here,' she says. 'I can set whole pages straight. Fit you all in, and make a future for myself. I put in whole brigades, of spear-throwers ...' and I say,

'You mean – spear-carriers,' and she says, no, hers are on the move, and in close order, not just trailing after.

Someone up there on the hill, the college, they reported it – Lara tells me how this guy, he closed his girlfriend up, maybe to possess her more, lessen the threat. Or just – his brain turned bad, like a cauliflower gone to mould. A horrible end for her. And his end too – full of little cadences. By law. Some trades – you can just lift people off the streets, and shut them in. No cadences, no calendars.

'You see?' says Lara. 'This arranging things. Is not just fantasy.'

'These little apartments,' I say, 'like those curiosity boxes that guy used to make, all incongruous, but neat, you can't have things and people spilling out the walls and windows.'

The cat food's ready – I say. 'Must we eat the same, all of us, cats too?'

'We are all one, that's what you always say,' she says. 'And it's convenient.'

'These felines—' I begin.

She interrupts: 'Whatever you're about to say, it makes no sense. So don't.'

I say, 'Look what's happening all over. It's revolution, round again. Here it comes, just like it didn't come when our parents longed for it, and hugged. This time – it's fucking monarchists and priests and such who cheer! Here, everybody wants a change that suits. Not to be left aside. Pretending to like guys indifferent to them, guys redrawing maps, guys having none. What's it all mean? Hot shards, these religions, dancing at our governors' legs, like shrapnel. Or else it's houses, made of sand, that's being built. Millions of them! What's behind it, Lara? What's coming down on us? Control? Torture, designed by law? It's all beyond me – here, I don't belong. I'm ignorant, and innocent.'

She stirs the pot: she says, 'I'm off quite soon. Protecting animals, since I haven't protected you ...'

I'm amazed. I say, 'Things here, they change. The guys that were marooned, up on their ladders – now they're looking bright, maybe they'll start to climb again.'

'So what,' she says. 'You never climbed. I think you like the snakes. Down there, you're on firm soil. It does you credit – with me, at least, but no one else.' I say,

'I bet for you the attraction was my stuff with criminals? And staring at the stars? With Claire too, the thief? Who steals from everyone? That's why you leave, and don't invite me too.'

Lara says, 'The trouble is – they're pillars of it all. Gangs, community, tattoos, and cutting throats. It's all too much the same, it's not outside us, it is exactly us. A different shade of grey, that's all. Our unthinking wills, they roam and squabble, plot and stab. It is exactly us.'

I'm impressed. I say, 'Well, even so, it has its fascination. We're supposed to love the everything, the all-around ...' She ladles out the catfood, says,

'You may, I don't. Now, say goodbye when Alma comes...'

And so I shall.

'Well, Alma,' I say. 'Making my own way again.'

'That's good, so good,' she says, taking off her shawl. I say,

'You look at the big things happening out there – the evolution of it all, when everything is made of similar materials, the universal stuff. You mustn't intervene, or if you do, you only nudge. But destiny – it's massive. The little stems and stalks that stick and swirl – you think they're huge – they are. But it's all details, it's all swept away. There's no design – it's just what is, and how it twists ...'

'His friends will beat you in the streets,' Lara tells Alma.

Alma looks bleak. I say,

'No, it's the profs. They're into distances you haven't paper you can write them down. And times – the same. The things that slither, then they hop, and then there's sludge again, or slush. And then there's sushi, then there's us.'

Alma peers at me. She says, 'Yes, yes – it's so. You see the art, and then the news, and guys that run from here and there, convinced. All going round, suffering by rote. And herding people, putting them in lines, and then there's nothing left to eat.'

'Alma tries to sort it out – is it a news sheet? Or some art?' Lara goes on, ignoring Alma but talking about her. 'She lost her families, but they never said quite why, if it was something that they did, or what she was. They kept it secret, but it shouldn't take a lot to work it out.'

'I have loss, that's quite a positive matter,' Alma says, 'And chaos.'

'Chaos or disorder?' Lara asks, quite sharply.

'Oh, chaos,' Alma says. 'I guess you could do poems – if you were a poet. It's quite irreversible, though. Loss.'

'Well,' I say, intruding, 'I've no pardon. Those profs – quite superficial. Proud of the good things they think their kids did with their guns. Me – the people I know with guns – they don't think they're doing good things.'

'I'm sure you could do politics as well,' says Alma, trying to take things in. 'Or little acts of justice.'

'Yes,' I say, 'if I was really into it. I think you must be ready for just anything. My friends don't vote. They don't go out and have the cops to billy them. But, yes, I see you think, "These guys, they're pretty much quite hopeless scum."'

Lara moves into a higher gear: 'You know, the forest where I'm off to save the animals – quite long ago, was densely populated. With humans. Now, it seems it's the domain of animals, but once – people. Villages. Towns and dancing. Then the other humans came.'

'Their viruses ...' adds Alma.

I say, 'My family – they had an imaginary member. They believed in him. They called him Michael Hove.'

'Alma gave all her money to a sect,' says Lara.

'It wasn't much,' says Alma. 'I was convinced, just then.'

'That's terrible,' I say.

My father would have given me advice: 'Drop that woman. Leave that country. Clean your mind.' It's good to have advice.

I stare at Alma – she wears those high dresses, like she's Amish, which she's not. Her skin – a line comes to me, 'spotty as a fig pudding'. When they torture you, maybe they fit another skin, when they have done – if ever they are done. Or maybe she's so white and pure, she doesn't let it out, her skin – forever shaded, remembering ancestral parasols against the sun at Biarritz. She must be fifty – nothing at all, when you think of stars. Stars in the sky, not in the circus. And all so long ago, the waves, the sea, long gone, flopped down, exhausted. My family: – Lara, they didn't like. In her own unliked way, they thought she was too good for me. Michael Hove, now – he could drive my parents where they wanted, at the right speed too. Relied on to weep when they were dead. Now, Michael Hove, writing down my thoughts, shaking his sad, his perfect, head.

There's been a long silence. I say, 'I did a course in aerial photography. I know all about it – I could be up there, filming Lara while she fosters cubs.'

'It's not just cuddles,' Lara says. 'It is a project, details minute, and balances exotic.'

'You need an aeroplane for those photos,' Alma says.

'A boss,' I say. 'That's what you need.'

'A platform,' Lara says. 'Everybody does.'

'You think there's one for everyone?' asks Alma. 'I'm sorry, the things I say are trite, but I am deep.'

'Of course, there's one,' says Lara. 'And you can't show there's not.'

'How I hope Claire will drop round,' Lara lies.

Claire – she's a sexual Parthenon – the spear, eternal flames, the giggling virgins. She's gathered so much wisdom ... Lara whispers to Alma, 'Claire is a thug.'

I say, 'It's true I've all the richness of new knowledge, but I can live like one of these,' and I put out my hand towards a cat.

'No,' says Claire. 'Your scraps of tittle, picked up in the bar – that isn't knowing anything. It's squalid. Doing courses when you need an aeroplane...' She has brought a bottle.

Lara says, 'Maybe I should make spaghetti?' Alma says,

'It's too early for spaghetti – not for a martini, though.'

'This bottle's not spaghetti, nor martinis either,' says Claire.

Lara says, 'Oh no, it's not a drinking party!'

'You know,' says Claire. 'Since Lara's off, and you will have to leave this pad as well,' she smiles at me, 'we could do a sledding, right across the country. Sponsored by some guys I know who need to clean some cash. The hard bits we could do by train – I know conductors everywhere.'

'I'd love to come,' says Alma, 'but the trains – maybe they won't take the dogs?'

'Then it's man's work,' Claire says. 'You'll have to pull, Alma. Like those old barge-haulers,' and she smiles at me. Then,

'Look, Alma, can we dump you off someplace?' she asks.

'Oh no,' says Alma pertly. 'I'll stick with you. I never criticise the company I'm with.'

'We could take a car, go see some grannies,' I suggest.

'My granny's in Haiti,' Claire says.

'I see you've taken over quickly, Claire,' Lara says. 'This guy – I couldn't stand him any more, you should watch out.'

'Well, you abandoned him, just like these cats, to go and coddle others,' Claire says, laughing to blunt the point, and Lara says,

'Those cats are smart. They'll not forget.' We ponder this, who's abandoned, who remembers.

'If I'd known we're into heavy conversation, I'd have brought another bottle,' Claire says.

Lara shows a nature movie. 'You're going to make a peace?' asks Alma. 'That's a noble thing. Those zebras and the crocodiles ...'

'The nasty ones – they get to eat the pretty things. It doesn't seem quite right,' I say.

Lara's irritated. 'That's how it is. That's why the movie's made.' I say.

'I know all that, I see it. Life. Or not. Lara, why don't you make the creatures food, like you give the cats and me? Then this eating thing would be resolved. And those poor guys that live in huts – they could get some too,' and Lara turns the movie off.

'Mine are tiny things,' she says. 'Almost like grit. And they eat nectar, maybe a puffball for dessert. They're almost invisible, no one gets to eat, or even see, them.'

'That's all right, then – go to, Lara!' Alma shouts.

I'm not convinced, I tell them how some stars, they may eat other stars, but there's no blood, no fuss, we hear about it, if at all, a million years to come, and Lara says, 'Oh no, not more stuff about the stars. If you're hungry – there's kilometres of spaghetti, just to hand.'

I put a record on, it's Hendrix, 'Up from the skies.'

We try to dance to it, Claire and I – 'Look, they're a zebra,' Alma laughs. 'All striped together, prancing there,' but Lara lies quiet, in wait.

All are quite merry, except Lara. Alma recites, 'past those two long spits of sand there stands the harbour wall, samphire and rock-cress making their show, the schooners elegant and rich unload the bales of spice and silk, and quincaillerie from Madagascar, while little skiffs race to and fro, the cormorants peering with one eye into the deeper blue, the other scanning for the clouds that come with the noon heat, and on the shore the merchants, the "blue ones", travelled from Maracaibo and from Tenerife stand majestic with their camels, daggers with crude rubies set into their pommels ...'

'What's all that?' asks Claire. 'Must be Stevenson. Or Conrad.'

'I remember everything he wrote,' says Alma, proudly.

Some guy comes in. He says, 'Hey! My motor! Someone's prised up the hood all round – maybe a tire iron ...'

'That red job?' I ask. 'Maybe it was me. Wanted to see who's it might be. A roadster, that's what they're called. They scare the cats – they hate the colour red.'

'The cats are all inside,' says Lara feebly. So they are.

'I came to say farewell,' the guy says. He feels he can't object too much. Politeness is a trap. Parked right outside, the nuisance, where I could see it ...

'You, guy! Wire wheels, red body!' says Claire. 'Who's leaving then?'

'I'm not,' says the guy. 'The motor's jammed.'

'It seems we're all leaving,' I say. 'That's what parties do. Farewell, farewell, and o remember me! A contradiction there...'

'I didn't mean it quite so hard, abandoning you all,' says Lara, crying.

'I'm sure we're used to it,' says Alma. 'Usually done with more style.'

'Well,' I say. 'Lara did the decent thing, eventually. She cried, as she was leaving.'

'You're quite perverse,' says Claire. 'And that silly car – they'll make you sweat for that.'

'His red rooster? Besides, Claire – that Alma, lost her family, now she has this tic, it all goes into literature and memorising. Print doesn't disappear. You didn't help.'

'She isn't sympa. She is rather dull,' says Claire. I say,

'Now – where's to go? Here we are. Now, that's a thing it's always possible to say, wherever you may find yourselves.' If you're in luck, I think, and living.

'Anywhere you run to,' Claire says. 'There'll be poor people, poorer than you can believe, and lots of cops that listen to the things you say. Especially you. You toss out words, not caring where they fall. The cops'll lock you up ...'

'Quiet, Claire! You bring up these poor people – it's your excuse for wanting far away from them,' I say. 'And making cash. And Lara – joining the animals, she will not resist and fight. The bad guys ramp around, waving their axes and their viruses – and all she thinks of is a spot where all can live in harmony. "Back to the garden, crock of milk of kindness for the snake ... My! the territory's smaller every day, so close the gate ... keep out the evil fruit ... put on your pants ..."'

'You should try focussing your anger,' Claire says.

Oh no, there's Alma.

'Here I am,' she says. 'My family gets better the longer it's been dead.'

'Mine had a store that fell on them,' Claire says. 'Better trust the street.'

'That's enough of families,' I say. 'Mine had no one to blame but themselves.'

Lara leaves to do her good work, restoring everything. The balance before the sin. All animals, disposed for our enjoyment and cuisine.

'If it wasn't for Alma here, we two could be a metal band,' Claire says to me, irritated. 'I have the voice, and you – the vision. You could strum something.'

Alma says, 'Now, my dears, believe me – metal bands beat dog-sledding when it comes to time spent dully on the road. But – I'll be with you as you cut your path. Be careful, though, should you invent religion, do politics, all that. It bites you on the nose. My families, remember ...'

'Alma's just a Tory,' Claire says. 'You see it in her dress. Hiding her scaly skin.'

'Everything's been tried,' I say. 'Guys with whiskers, guys with beards, and guys without. Now, the empty space, dead genes. The void, the disappeared. All over. Nothing's left – maybe I'll be Michael Hove, example to you all.'

'I think before I act,' says Claire. 'Although that may not work. But you – you only think in afters.'

'The consequences is what you live with, Claire. Maybe we should go where it's still hot, and starting over, trying everything again,' I say.

'Enough!' says Claire. 'I'm your angel, that is true – but, as a glance will tell – I'm the black kind. Now, I'll tell you of my plan, and if you tell on me, or my associates, your brain will turn

to soup – but have no fear, the sexual bond between us is a band
of steel. You always wondered how it was that mind came out of
matter. Well, I'll tell – at least what's good for you. It's magic!
Now reflect, and don't come back with silly questions. And of
course – you know that Lara went with that odd guy whose car
you trashed, that Rudy? He was her cavalier ...' and I repeat,

'I know, I know,' although I don't.

'Hey now!' shouts Claire. 'This shouldn't be! Here's Lara,
banging at the door.'

And here she is: 'I went and then came back,' she says. 'It
often happens so. My animal is dead, extinct. In books, you just
arrive in time. Rudy and I – we had a little break for oldtime sex,
and then they said, "It has expired. The chain of life – the spiral
... it is broke."'

'That isn't anything,' says Claire, in command. 'Those
profs my lover, this guy here, was chatting with – they'll
supercharge our genes, and land some junk on planets far away,
where apples grow, and grass and stuff. We'll colonise the
galaxy, put a metre on our arms and legs ... that's what those
guys were saying over lunch...'

'No, no!' says Lara. 'No food. That is the message. My
small creature, scorpionlike, that pollinated things – without him
and his complicated ways, the copulations in a mystic knot, the
colour coding and the poison spots – without all that, within a
year, there'll be no food, no buds, no birds, no animals of any
kind: amusement and use, they're at an end. The brick that kept
the mansion tall – is crumbled, dead. Extinct.' Maybe she weeps.

'Oh come,' says Alma. 'Don't exaggerate.'

'Those rockets they send up,' I say. 'It's clear, they're
packed with people, a getaway – landing all over on stars and
stuff. Colonies and empires. With no food.'

'They'll all be having babies – those trips are long,' says Lara. 'Just imagine – all your life spent in a speeding tube, your destiny to procreate.'

Rudy's come along. He chimes in, 'Sure, no moral education there.'

'Well, Rudy,' Lara says, and clings to him. 'I guess the sex we'll have should last us to the end, not start to pall, or send us off to stranger doings ...'

'Hey, greedy guys!' I say. 'This news – extinction – has come so many times before. The individual, fearing death, transforms it into communal expiring,' though starvation's banal and lengthy. There's more drama, being burned up by the sun.

'There's bargains in all this,' says Claire: 'Just think! The things to buy up! What they call subsets will corner markets ... Although, to watch the more unfortunate, less provident, pass on, that's die, will make a painful scene.'

'All those murders, stretching back,' Alma says. 'It makes it nonsense, and it makes it sense. The sense is nonsense, if you understand ...'

'You're crazy,' Claire says. 'No one will die, and all will suffer as they do, and all, well, yes, will die, but not because of Lara's scorpion. Just contemplate our species, its accomplishments, its goals, maybe its deficiencies ...'

There's the angel in her talking, and Rudy says he'd rather fix his car than frowst around in Lara's bed all day.

It's like a Japanese library – full of books you can't read, you're sightless, mute, even the exit sign's a mystery.

Rudy – red all over, quivering like a boxer – hits me once, below an eye. He's hurt his hand, and 'There!' he says. For Lara, or the car. No consequences, not even justice.

196

'To show that we don't care,' says Claire, 'we must have a feast.'

'There's just potatoes left,' says Lara, and we sit and wait. The last cat, Flower, is bibbed and sat beside.

'Where'd the other moggies go?' I ask.

'They went to barbecues,' says Lara.

'It never comes to being cannibals,' Alma says. 'That's maybe a mistake. I was never taught at school – it seems that's a tabu,' and as we contemplate, and Rudy pinches Flower's thigh, and then, in fun, he pinches Alma's too – we think of who's more appetising. I say to Claire, 'This sex bond we have – does it involve some acts?'

'Oh no,' she says. 'For they would spoil and complicate. Look in my eyes – ' and then I do, and see the table and the sacrifice, the souls that's taken out and bottled, the voices in the stone, and think – 'Better all that than fumbling in some bed, or scrunched in Rudy's sporty little car.'

'Here it comes!' shouts Lara, and what munificence we see! Potatoes dauphine, croquette: potatoes Port-au-Prince, *à l'irlandaise*, Bolivian deep-frozen, trampled underfoot, and sweet, and sour, those crunchy straw-like things, and frites of every calibre, potatoes big as Swedish heads, tiny as stripy marbles, from Courland and from Kiev, in stew and powder – Rudy says he always keeps some in the car, packets of potato dust, you just add water, there you are: – potatoes pinked and curried, peppered à la Red Queen, smoked and whipped ...

We eat until we gag, we pause, and eat and eat, and gag again.

Alma says, 'Maybe we should keep to plant anew,' and Lara says no, no, without the sting that impregnates they'll just lie down and rot, and even Flower licks a drop, the conversation tingles – even better than the talk of rocketry and hunters killing tigers on the steppe.

And the vodka. Yes, the vodka, not to forget the vodka.

'You pulled off Rudy's ear,' the scream is Lara's, and I echo Alma, say –

'Don't exaggerate. It's just a part of the external part. An impulse, nothing more. It was his talk of moral training, in the rocket, as it speeds for centuries, to plant our seed in some hot, steamy star. For that's a place, the rocket tube, where there's no good or bad, no deed foresworn or done. No reflection and no impulse.'

'And that's what Rudy said,' she screams at me. 'You cretin!'

Most of us are drunk. 'I shall not leave the life, before I've had my say,' I say with dignity. 'Morality is still a thing I cherish, and I seek,' and I hug Alma. She's the best of all of them. I shall protect.

'Confront big themes, settle small scores,' I say, and Alma says,

'Right on! That's what makes history history.'

Rudy's ear looks like a spigot, and it pours like one. The blood is more to Flower's taste than spud. We laugh at that. Remembering his ear, will make his righteousness a comic turn.

'Really, we shouldn't laugh,' says Alma, laughing. 'Not at misfortunes – but there's so many of those, there'd be little else left for laughter ...'

'That wasn't a misfortune,' Lara says, though it won't affect their sexuality, I'd suspect.

'You go on and laugh,' says Claire hugging Alma. 'I shall die rich and laughing if I can.'

'We've feasted. Now we should dance,' I say. 'But not to Hendrix. I always cry when I hear these songs and wish I'd been born a Catalan.' We talk of music. When we've all starved, where will be the music then? It's true, we'll understand the fate of our unhappy, hungry comrades, all around the world – but music! Where will that all go?

'It's written down,' says Alma, 'some of it. And that will blow around. The rest – it comes from bones, to bones it will return,' and we are sombre, while I pick a disc.

'Tristan!' I say, and Lara says it's not for dancing to, and anyway worn thin with hearing over – but I'm indifferent, I just want to hug with Claire, maybe I'll die rich with her ...

'You know,' says Alma, as I look for music than can fit our feet, 'Lara's scorpion sets us free! We don't need now to shoot and burn and stretch each other. There's no point, next year, we'll all be dead, or agonising. Now we can think what questions we should like to solve,' but Claire strokes me, says, 'Hold on – I need this guy as muscle in my plan. He's got no cash, so simple soldiering's his fate ...'

I say, 'But Claire, there is the sexual bond, and politics as well, no doubt the post-colonial sympathy we share...'

'Yes, yes,' she says, 'there's lots of philosophical stuff to do – but my associates will surely want to put their cash in things that keep them hanging on when all the rest have given up. That means they'll want aggression too.'

'No, Claire,' Lara says. 'I'm sure when all is lost, you'll join the sad brigades,' and Claire turns away, and Alma says when music's lost, and we can dance no more – where's literature, its consoling, like they say it does?

Alma starts reciting: 'I had done a few things and earned a few pence, my family was murdered for no crime, and now I

199

find myself, quite drunk, with petty criminals and people arrogant, depressive, and yet I need to chronicle past deeds, relying on my obvious fitness for the task – what happened to my grannies – and, additionally, my general perceptive possession of a scene that's new – the imminent, definitive elimination of the human race ...'

'Alma, that's very nice, and clever too – but do you really hope to add to what is over, half-forgotten?' asks Lara.

We dance, Claire and I, like bugs who've fallen on the stove. The music comes from inside, probably it is different for each. That doesn't seem a difficulty.

'Alma,' Lara insists, 'if you write down your history, will anyone be there to read it? And then again, when things are nearly at an end, they don't relent, those guys, they like to see opponents killed. These are all things to take into account,' and she smiles kindly, then she says, 'I'll ask my Rudy – he's a kind of priest or guru, he will surely know how we should behave ourselves,' and Claire shouts, 'It's only us that knows the ending, and it's only Lara who has told us what it is,' and that is true, though we're convinced.

'Lara, you do believe all this, what you have told?' I ask.

'Of course it's true. An off-print, would that do, convince?' she asks. 'It's just the favour that I did, that you would be the first to know.'

We do a general dance, a swaying on the spot. It's more about the misery to come than comradeship. The others – seem to have thick lives, and contradictions. What is my life? What was it?

What will it be like, no food, no trek to camps, no state, no fighting for the sack of flour, no rights abused?

'Poor Rudy,' Lara says, 'he is so red. And after sex, he almost dies, his pumps are clogged.' There, who could resent a guy like that?

'When I was in the jungle,' Lara says. 'And they told me we were done for – it occurred to me: design. It couldn't be intelligent, if the failure of one tiny part could bring down all the rest. But, sure, it's all design. And so I thought – a new arrangement. No more hierarchy, no tower of being. Discontinuity. Poor Rudy – even his feet are red. There's one alternative for me: Rudy. And you – you're another. Absorb them both. That way I can be committed to you both, and not depend ...'

'You always went in for arranging, but this one's not for me,' I say. 'Rudy – what does he think?'

'Oh, he thinks a lot,' she says, 'but he's no plan. He has his faith – if it's wrong, he'll be quite lost.'

'Maybe if he bursts while you two have your sex, he wouldn't even need to know the truth or not, the right and wrong?' I say. 'We have to plan,' she says, 'now that there's no future waiting.'

Claire says, 'I'll have you meet my friends. They are Ukrainians, mostly. They won't like you. They will think you're trash. But don't despair – you're in my frame. Better an end complete, than economics going wrong that lasts for years. Of course, knowing what awaits, there's no point in a long relationship – I'm sure we're both relieved,' and so we are.

Alma prepares to write – she's not sure what: 'Once, they said, to serve the people. Now, we shall starve with them,' she says. Yes, Alma is the best, I'd cling to her.

'We've done the dance,' says Lara, 'and that will do. Now, we must do the monument.'

'I think,' I say at once, 'it should be music. That will last for ever.'

'No one will be there to hear,' says Rudy.

'That's always irrelevant, when music is around,' I say.

'If we do a statue, no one will be there to see it either,' Alma says. We think more deeply.

Claire says, to hurry things along,

'Rudy's quite an ordinary guy. We cover him with clay, and that's a mould. We put more clay inside – there's then two Rudy's, one dead, one clay, when all is done. And that's the type. "Man". No numen. No celebrating what isn't there.'

'I think,' says Alma, twisting her notebook, 'it should be an open space. Quite fastidiously clean. No bones or diaries, and no grass. Just a place you can't tell what happened there, or what's to come. No tired mementoes, and no stones.'

'No, no,' says Lara, 'that is way depressing. No, none of that. It mustn't be vainglorious, but not defeat and sad. No nullity.'

Are we close? We shall all watch each other die.

'Look at Flower,' says Lara. 'She's becoming quite human.'

She's on a shelf, staring at us, like she was a book you'd need to read.

'OK,' says Rudy, 'that can be your place,' and she jumps off. A yellow cat with orange eyes.

Later, Lara takes me aside: 'Look, Rudy's keen on that idea from Claire – a memorial to him, his ego. I am not. There's only one thing we can leave, I feel. A space.'

I say, 'I know! It's "Lara's scorpion".'

'Exactly so,' she says. 'In malachite. There's lots up on that mountain, you and Claire, you can climb ...'

202

'Hmmm,' says Claire, 'malachite. Ukrainians are used to mining it. It's as good a thing to own as any. There's some tooled in on Alma's escritoire.'

I say, 'Come on, Claire, climb the mountain with me. Keep me quiet, and Lara too.'

Claire says 'The best thing to leave behind, if you can't leave behind a sea, is a palace. No one will live in it, but in many palaces they don't, or else someone lives there who didn't build. I see the stucco – and the gold, like butter icing. I'd have it made of chocolate, with sugar, green and white and gold. And on the top, those cherries, if we can't have stars ...' We're all hungry, Claire most of all, for cake. Lara says,

'Stars, Claire. Don't mention them. Quite out of register. I'm more modest – I'd have Flower, set on a plinth. She's come quite near to us – that must show something?'

Claire sighs, 'We don't do things together now, processions, funerals, and weddings, everything that's in between. The cat – she's come in at the tail end.'

'I didn't know about your passion for cake, Claire,' I say. 'It's quite endearing.'

'Forget the cake part,' she says. 'It's palaces, the thing.'

We climb the copper mountain. At the top, driving me on – fish pie, and pears in caramel.

'Two things I can't abide,' says Claire. 'Pears and pie. And the fish?'

'It's when they're left to suffocate,' I say. 'Even sheep have it better – but in the pie, the fish are done with suffering.'

We haul each other up. I shout, 'Claire, the chain that broke – the planet can't have been so fine, so balanced, tested ...'

She shouts back, 'It never needed explanations, even less now, when ...' We struggle on.

'The lumps of malachite. How big?' I ask.

'Another silly question,' Claire says, tossing rocklike things. 'Enough it's green, red-spotted, like the scorpion. This stuff – will need some treatment.'

When we reach the top, a panorama – there'll be the Orient. The steppe. The sea of Aral that blows its poisonous dust over mankind.

'Aggression without power, it's quite so trivial,' pants Claire.

'Most people manage just with that,' I say.

'Sure,' she says, 'but we want something special. This copper heap – we've a bent trader, metals exchange, all that. We'll find a corner, then we're in for life.'

It seems a little thing. I say, 'I thought I might be salaried, and help you steer a course.'

She says: 'As for you, I have my doubts. You're not cut out to do crime seriously. Not anything. Egocentric is the word.'

'When do we arrive,' I ask, 'at the top?'

'Oh,' she laughs. 'You'll no doubt get fish pie.'

I say, 'The big guys, in big countries, if they apologised for everything, they'd never stop. Alma says they should sit with shaven heads, like monks with begging bowls that's full of spit, on street corners in the rain.'

'Alma has her burdens,' Claire says. 'Remember, you must stand the object against itself, or else you couldn't see it. That should be clear.'

'It's not at all,' I say.

She says, 'The telescope – to make a distant thing seem near – if you just looked along a tube, that would be magic. But it's not. Because you make another little image upside down, imaginary – and then you see.'

'It's all about my pay, it seems,' I say. 'At least, we're still good friends, my dear?'

'Of course,' she says. 'It's just we need a dull and stable guy, a punk. Not you. And as for telescopes, it works for salaries and history. To make a job worthwhile, you need that little image, tiny and invisible. That's cash. With history, you bring it near – but no one lives again, and nothing moves. You see,' and she heaves me up, her shoulders straining at my buttocks, 'in a hundred years, all will be fine and prosperous. But with the violence, you need power, and that's your image, do you see.'

We change around, I heave her up. 'Yes,' I say, 'I'm following your argument. Though if it's true, that's quite another thing.'

'Without the following, you would never have the truth,' she says.

It's like the cafeteria and the profs. The distances, up from the skies, the dancing genes, and Lara, queenly, when she had her flock of cats.

Then there's the copper dust. We sink in it, immobilised. At night they pour some more, Claire's poor castle's covered. Then the rains will set it hard. We're stuck, till Claire says, 'Dance. That's the thing. I'll teach you steps ...' and so she does. We wriggle out, and then we're down. The stacks of malachite, the grey stones, they are all around, the monument can be begun.

Around there's lines of folk: I ask, 'Is it for bread? Or for a lifetime, rocketed towards some patch of turf a million years away?'

Someone says, 'They're off to Saturn, there, they will decide where to go next.' They do not talk of scorpions.

There's other lines, of altruists – they make up little gene packs, so if anyone survives, I guess, they'll loop in selections of our finest guys.

'It makes your violence, your aggression, seem pathetic now,' says Lara. 'And Rudy's quite worn out – although no doubt he'll leave his tattered genes for what comes next.'

'My memoir,' Alma says. 'There are so many culpable. My family dodged around, and suffered from their choice. Their torment came not by chance, or nature either, but I don't know where to start. It's all been said before, the politics, but if you leave it out, there's just your friends that's on the scene ...'

'You don't have time for quibbling, Alma,' Claire says. 'Of course it's all been done before. You write it down again, you start with the Romanians, and then go on. This time, with Lara's scorpion – no state, no history's to blame, they'll say. Though maybe if she'd got there earlier, she might have found the creature still alive... So, Alma, no justice then or now. The chain of being holds until it snaps – there's nothing to be done. Just write things down, and we'll decide the way to take them. A memoir. Even if you don't remember it.'

Alma writes, 'Today the chief engineers have been down to our part of the mine. The management has issued some instruction or other about boring new galleries, and so the engineers arrived to make the initial survey. I checked the woodpile behind our little house, and moved a nest of mice to where our cat, Flower, could not reach them. I had sent the children far away, for with hostilities afoot, prudence is required. Then I heard the neighbour whisper to me, "There's soldiers coming down the road. For sure, they are not ours."'

'That's my grandfather,' Alma says, doubtfully. 'They were Romanians, the soldiers.'

'You never forget a word you've read, Alma,' says Lara, part proud, part doubtfully.

'No blood, no jackals,' Alma says. 'I have to hurry, set it all down. What good comes from this?'

'What do you get from all this, Lara? I ask. 'Watching us like gladiators, preparing to die?'

'You must find yourselves. And be yourselves,' she says.

'That's two things, Lara,' I say, 'which don't fit.'

She holds Flower, vertical, like a wriggling infant: she says, 'I love you all, in different ways. You must succeed, before it is too late.'

'You mean,' I say, 'when it is too late. I'm nothing. Against this obstacle, elimination, you can't do anything. No food, no energy. Some things explode, and others cool right down. Rudy is ice, Claire and me – we're hot blobs.'

'I love you, anyway,' she says briskly.

'Unfortunately, Lara,' I say, 'you're dead.' Like Alma. Claire – just stirring on, being what she's made to be, though her story isn't interesting, not enough for Alma to make it up. Grand fraud, it's called, her speciality, her crime. And so,

'There's little time,' I say. 'I'm going to make the break. Here's what I propose. A future not born from the past, that's what should come after us. Not helping people catching up with richer guys. Not killing off the guys who won't enjoy the future that you make for them. Not killing off the ones that don't agree, or look suspicious.'

Lara says, 'I didn't tell too many people, about the scorpions. There didn't seem a point. What's going to happen – it will happen anyway.' She hasn't understood. I say,

'What there will be, when we are gone, is not my inventions. Only the best, there'll be. But things you can't imagine. Not legacies: – the best.'

'It makes no sense,' says Lara. 'It sounds quite infantile.'

'Sense?' I say. 'Where's the sense in other galaxies we'll never reach? And those dead ancestors?'

'It's like a kingdom of the gods, your afterworld,' says Lara, humouring. 'Life in the sun, the shadows disappeared. Perfection unimaginable.'

'Like maybe what goes on on other stars?' I ask, 'or planets?'

'You must spend more time on saying what you mean,' she says.

'I can't say more – you must see that.'

I'm witness in a trial – the guy whose story I took down, and then he cut his girl. I don't know what will happen to him. I can guess.

'Who will bury us, Lara?' I ask. 'We can expect no justice either.'

'Oh, we'll all help, I'm sure,' she says.

'Rudy should carve the monument, the scorpion,' I say.

'Oh yes,' says Lara. 'Poor Rudy. With him, it's all platonic now. He's weakening – but sculpting helps him find himself. We didn't see the cache of malachite that Claire threw down – but there's enough on Alma's escritoire to make a tiny, life-size one...'

I say, 'My prof, that guy – I hear he went to Titan, one of Saturn's moons. There's methane lakes. And methane ice and methane rain.'

'Well, yes, that figures,' Lara says, 'with lakes of methane, you'd need ice and rain the same. I hope he didn't quote me when he left ...'

'Oh no,' I say, 'he'll launch himself again from there. He'll start a dynasty, like pharoahs did – he'll breed in rockets, those will be his pyramids, and so his genes will land up on some planet wandering, quite unaware, his kids will found an empire, culture too ...'

'The vision is a noble one,' says Lara, not convinced. 'You don't seem to have the detail right.'

That guy's trial – he needs, if not an alibi, then stories. I tell them about Indians, and I think of how with them, Lara's scorpion might have been a totem, venerated, or at least not left to die. The guys in court – it seems they think I'm on a trip. It doesn't help my friend. I whisper to him – 'In a year or so, it will be done and finished, though each of us will have to bury all their friends ...' I try to comfort him, but there's no space ... I'm ushered out. Some justice will get done, to him.

Claire says, 'We don't care if it's true. Apocalypse. We bet against it, and we bet the other way as well. We'll make some cash, and if we don't – another Lara, another ending of the world will come along. And when it does, we shan't collect, for sure, but nor will we pay out.'

I should have had my gang, and ordered guys around, and done some deals, repented, maybe, given cash to charities. Or else – been Michael Hove, and driven people round, so carefully. The hunger – always with you, slides its paw in yours. Maybe Claire – she has a source of food, and in a chamber secretly, tears off wings and legs, and stuffs them down, the bones, the plumes. Rudy hammers at his car. His face is grey. I say, 'That monument: – the beast is tiny, and malformed.' He says, offhand, 'If there are things come after we have gone – it's probable they're small and malformed too.'

'Don't let him go!' shouts Lara, as he speeds away: 'There's so much work needed to be done on him.'

'He couldn't take the hunger, Lara. That's what drove him off,' I say.

'He may crash himself,' says Lara. 'That silly car. He's suffering so – he ought to end it. And, you know, he couldn't stand you.'

'Yes, I know,' I say. 'It's not surprising.'

'We could all have gone on trips,' she says.

'Lara,' I say, 'your trips end bad. Look what you didn't bring us back.'

She turns on me, 'You needn't believe me, if it is too hard. I want nothing from you. But you'll know, the pain, the longing. It beats anything that Alma writes about.'

'Oh, I agree,' I say. 'I need no further proof. It's all uphill – the copper mountain, made of dust, my record with the cops, the gossip. Nothing's easy now.'

'At least you went to court,' she says: 'You were a citizen.'

'It wasn't up to me,' I say, 'The guy who cut her up, his girl, the Indian – he couldn't tell us why.'

Does Claire have food, I ask myself, black markets work better than the ones they talk about on television, those that failed. 'Claire doesn't love you,' Lara says. 'She just hoped you'd steal some buns....'

Later:

'We shouldn't sit and wait,' I say to Claire, referring to the end, and tell her about Rudy.

'Oh, it's jealousy,' she says. 'Or just to get away.'

'There isn't anywhere to go,' I say. 'You have to wait the drama out – or else ...'

'Or else it isn't drama,' Claire agrees. 'No one is trustworthy. No one is after you. They say it's sickness, this suspicion – but I am in the midst of it, I promise you, no suspicion is misplaced.'

'It's not like Alma's folks,' I say. 'They were harassed out of everywhere.'

'That part – it hasn't happened here, not yet,' she says. 'Rudy went off to look for food. Maybe you should do the same.'

'I ought to be the fool,' I say, 'the saviour, the innocent – it can only be me, but it doesn't fit. The quest is always for the grail, for purity, for as-it-was. Not burgers.'

I think how the profs... they ran. They couldn't mend it, but they knew the time was up. Where's the food been stacked, I wonder – climb the mountain, soft with chocolate powder. Up and over. See where Rudy's smashed his red machine.

'We ought to fix things,' Claire says. 'That's what we're famous for.'

'We understand the chain of being, Claire,' I say. 'I heard it over lunch. It's we don't know how to fix, though lots must be responsible. The strange thing is, Lara's our messenger.'

'The messenger but not the news,' she says.

'Of course,' I say. 'We should have known to plant some seeds.'

'That's so simple, you must know it doesn't work like that,' says Claire.

'Music ho!' I shout. 'Let's keep our dignity and dance!' I put on 'Ready for the Hit between the Eyes', we dance, Claire and I, separately. It goes quite well.

Alma comes in, she says, 'My memoir is finished. Now, I'll dance with Flower – she's ugly, just like me.' Alma is the best, she's wild, she's heavy, she is light. We are all light, with our not eating.

Flower looks like a teddy bear, the coat, the stare. 'See!' Alma says, 'what does it take to make her civilised?'

'I guess we'll sit around and die?' I say. 'That's nothing new – but, with you guys, it's peppery too.'

'We're all too weak for sex,' says Lara, though she's not been thinking in that way. 'Poor Rudy – he got tired of repetition. That's the artist for you. He didn't sculpt too well.'

'I shan't hang around for long,' says Claire. 'We've found a stash of spoons and forks. The cache of food – it can't be far away. If we don't eat it all, I'll share it out. That's communism, my dears – sharing the poverty around.'

'Yes,' Alma says, 'it's always politics, at the end as well. I wonder why poor Rudy was so red?'

'It wasn't genes,' says Lara, irritably, 'probably to match his automobile.'

'Maybe he knew about the spoors, the hunting?' Alma pushes on. 'Was he a red man, gathering archaic things upon the icy steppe? Whittling the rocks? The reddest Indian, last Mohican? Seen it so often, yet we didn't recognise ...'

'Cut the crap, Alma, please,' says Lara, much incensed: 'Maybe he came from Mars – they're all red there, as we all know, and maybe brought his motor too. He's just a loser. Arm-wrestling was for him the tops.'

'We don't expect carvers to be bright,' I say, thinking of the guy who cut his girl. And carving joints ... 'Or smoking them,' says Alma, pertly. 'They say it's good for appetite.'

'Flower's awful thin,' says Lara, pinching her, and changing tack. 'There's not a slice of meat on her.'

There's a rattling. We look out. It's Rudy's car, for sure, and all opinions, theories have to be revised. Oh no! It isn't Rudy after all – 'It's Flower!' says Claire.

'She purrs!' says Alma. 'It is transformation! She could be Parsifal – except ... I don't feel anything.'

It is a little miracle. Alma says, '"It is the best time we have ever had! said Frederick ..." oh, who said that, I wonder. Who was Frederick? But how apposite, it must be French. This moment – how many people out there who won't share. My book is full of them ...' She weeps. We could all weep, but don't.

'Come, come, Alma,' Claire says, though not liking her a sliver more. 'The fascists came, and then they went. They're just a speck on someone's broom. You can't blame them for the scorpion.'

Alma mumbles that the fascists passed the uniforms to other guys. I say, we're shut in here, and if they're all round, we shall not let them in. 'You're kind to say it,' Alma says. 'But my memoir – it's full of them, all sorts.'

'They're shut up in your book,' says Claire roughly. 'And you should shut up too. Alma, we're terminal in here. Rudy came from Mars, so now we know, and he was Lara's love, and he's gone back, no doubt, up there, down there. Food, Alma! Write me some food!'

'They're all gone now, and I can't ask them anything,' says Alma, weeping.

'Don't be such a baby, Alma,' Claire shouts – 'It's not you that suffered all that stuff, it's us that's suffering now.' Then she turns on me, 'This creep! And his creepy friends! The big time that he wanted – just being a DJ, spinning his platters, goofing off. And Lara coddling with her Martian, then off on mission, letting that creepy insect slip away, and all our food go with it – every loaf, the flat ones, raisin-filled, the twisted shiny ones, the baguettes, *rosette*, salt and bland, with seeds, with olives, sweet and oiled – all now expired. Goddamit, those sugar dragonflies – Lara, couldn't you find that little creature, in your shoe, or up your leg, some kind of asp, stuck in your bra – there's millions, bunches of eggs with legs that's sticking in your hair ... But no, "He's gone. the dear extinct. Departed, unwanted first, though now desired." You parasites! You stingless crawlers!'

'It's all self-hatred, dear, that rant,' says Lara, pacifying.

They grapple and scratch.

'No knives, dears,' Alma shouts. 'Look! Flower is frightened,' and indeed she is. She scratches too, but at the door.

I'm lucky, I hallucinate:

In Rudy's car, we're down the road that looks like food – the potholes look like empty oyster shells, red gravel's paprika, there's beetles crawling in our path, like capsicums. Those bushes, made of candied fruit, those mustard-coloured birds – I say to Rudy, 'Let's stop, enjoy the scene,' but no, he turns away, he's cherry-red all over, and he says, 'Not now, I must be back to Lara, for she loves me, there's no time to stuff the landscape down. It's true the streams are claret, but sobriety's the thing – I'm part of Lara's scene, I can't be late.'

'What, Rudy, exactly do you do?' I ask.

'Oh,' he says, 'I'm always there on time. I'm very punctual – ladies just love that. Five meals a day, and I am up for every

one, I don't say no, my body burns and burns, I'm like an oven,
what I eat is turned to crimson embers ... all turned to muscle,
and to steel – this sporty car is what I ate, I made a shell, just
like a lobster or a crab, and I go skeetering from side to side ...'
And so he does – the curry powder's loose, we slide, we almost
hit those quails, he brakes, we spin, beneath the gravel-paprika
we see rows of eggs – from plovers, eagles, guillemots and such
... He hits me, in the eye, above where he struck before. It stings.
And he drives off ...

'Hey, creepy guy, so you've come back from there!' It's
Claire, she's won her bout with Lara – 'No cheesy dreams from
you,' she says to me. 'You'd better find some food for Flower
that even in extremes we wouldn't eat.'

Lara says, 'Now, even with the Americans and their
bombs, their money – there's no recriminations. We're all in the
same basket now.'

We don't reply. There's nothing much to say. Then, Lara
screams at Alma,

'You didn't let Flower out! Not in the street, the
neighbours, all those folk ...!'

Alma's distressed: 'I thought it a good turn. Freedom, you
know. Escape.'

'You idiot!' says Lara. 'Rudy's gone, now Flower ...'

'Oh, they come back,' says Claire, quite unconcerned, and
tells a story of a cat that did.

'It isn't going right,' says Lara. 'I thought to have you all
around, for comradeship. In these hard times – you need a
plenitude, a raft. To say the world would end because I couldn't
sort my preferences out ... absurd!'

Claire says, 'Lara, I'm a cat that loves the street. There's
sure to be a crew somewhere, some guys who've seen it all, and

planned. But – one last time: Lara, you're sure it's as you say, the hunger's doing for us all, for you, and this guy here,' and she hugs me and smiles, 'There's really nothing, no way out, except some chance...?'

'No, Claire,' says Lara. 'There's no chance. And do you think I'd play a game, a trick, and sit here while you starve, like poor people that you see in photos do? No, I have told you how it is, exactly so.'

Claire goes out: she says, 'I'll look out for the cat. And you,' she says to me, 'you never were the tough and trusty guy you thought you were, the kind that hard guys want. It's quite a compliment.'

'Oh Claire,' I start to say, but Alma takes my arm. 'I did an awful thing,' she says. 'I hoped to see the people in my book, some I remember, others we have photos of – go out the door in time. Escape, and have another life, just like the cats.'

Alma goes to another room.

I say, 'Lara, it's stifling in here.'

'It must be Alma and her stove,' she says. 'They used to lie on it, the whole family, all year long, they say.'

'I'll take some air,' I say.

'You were a valid part,' she says to me, 'but you were there to be reformed a bit. Rudy – he was quite another thing. I had to sort things out. I'm still unsure.'

No, I shall never be the perfect driver, perfect son, a Michael Hove. I say,

'I appreciate you Lara, for what you might have done for me, if there had been time.'

I run outside. I hope I'll see Claire – there's no one there, outside.

I walk part way up the hill, the copper mound. No, you can't see the steppe, just a town, the walls toast-coloured, pale and burnt, every shade of hasty making or forgetfulness. No olives on the trees, no sheep, no bells. No people, just the hunger, in the head, like grit, no food.

A call to prayer comes feebly up the slope. I settle back.

Alma's the best.

I'm glad she isn't here.

There's movement in the sand. A little school of scorpions, it seems. They run, they play, they fence. Some are green, red-spotted, like the malachite.

THE END

About the author

John Fraser has lived in Rome since 1980. Previously, he worked in England and Canada.